"I _wanted_ to be on this case.

It wouldn't have been long before I'd have demanded it. Yeah, I knew Larry, but I didn't know him well enough to lose my objectivity. Don't blame yourself for that."

"Then I showed up, looking like trouble. You had to run around to try to prevent me from going ballistic all over the county."

At that, a small laugh escaped Cat. "It hasn't been that difficult."

"Because you were willing to work with me. But I'll be honest, much as I hate to admit it, when I arrived here I did want to tear a few people apart. Obviously, I didn't know who."

She raised a brow. "Do you still want to?"

"Tear someone apart? Sometimes, but the urge isn't as strong as when I arrived here. I think you'd be safe not worrying about that."

She squeezed his hand again, then withdrew hers. Duke regretted the absence of her touch immediately. Damn, he was starting to get tangled up between grief, anger and the pull he felt toward Cat.

CONARD COUNTY JUSTICE

New York Times Bestselling Author

RACHEL LEE

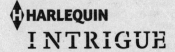

HARLEQUIN
INTRIGUE

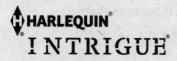

Recycling programs for this product may not exist in your area.

ISBN-13: 978-1-335-13646-6

Conard County Justice

Copyright © 2020 by Susan Civil Brown

This edition published by arrangement with Harlequin Books S.A.

For questions and comments about the quality of this book, please contact us at CustomerService@Harlequin.com.

Harlequin Enterprises ULC
22 Adelaide St. West, 40th Floor
Toronto, Ontario M5H 4E3, Canada
www.Harlequin.com

Printed in U.S.A.

Rachel Lee was hooked on writing by the age of twelve and practiced her craft as she moved from place to place all over the United States. This *New York Times* bestselling author now resides in Florida and has the joy of writing full-time.

CAST OF CHARACTERS

Cat Jansen—Deputy with the Conard County sheriff's office. She is an experienced investigator.

Major Daniel Duke—Army ranger, he is hunting his brother's murderer.

Larry Duke—The victim. An investigative journalist who had come to Conard County to write a book.

Ben Williams—Larry's boyfriend, former army officer, acquaintance of Daniel Duke.

Man 1, Man 2 and Man 3—Former military, Larry Duke's killers.

Chapter One

Cat Jansen was sitting at the front desk in the Conard County Sheriff's Office when trouble came through the door.

Rotation had brought her to this day of desk duty in the office. She wasn't expecting to be too busy, which was one of the reasons she had decided to stay in this county after her mother's death two years ago.

She had previously worked for a sheriff in Colorado but had left the job to come to Conard City to care for her ailing mother. Cancer was a brutal disease, and all Cat could say for the months she'd spent nursing her was that her mother hadn't been alone. Then she'd taken a job as a deputy to the sheriff here. Today she busied herself with a day of paperwork and a few relatively minor complaints.

Until the big guy in an Army uniform walked through the door. She took a rapid inventory as best she could. Major's oak leaves, a stack of colorful ribbons. He pulled off a tan beret as he entered.

His dark eyes reflected cold anger. More worrisome than rage, the coldness suggested a determination that wouldn't quit. *Oh heck*, she thought. What had made this guy look like this?

"Are you the desk officer?" he asked in a deep voice, suggesting a rumble of thunder in the distance.

"Yes, I am." An imposing man. And whatever had brought him so far out of his way was likely a serious problem.

"I'm Major Daniel Duke. My brother, Larry, was murdered a week ago."

Well, that explained the steel in his dark eyes. "I'm so sorry," she replied. "How can we help you?" But she had an idea. Definitely trouble. She could feel it brewing like a building storm.

"I want to know how the investigation is going."

"It's going." She wasn't permitted to give him confidential details of an ongoing investigation.

"Are you checking into the possibility of a hate crime? My brother was gay."

A bald accusation phrased as a question. If she hadn't felt so disturbed and chilled by the look in his eyes, she might have done more than sigh.

"Of course we are," she answered. "I knew Larry. We're not overlooking anything, believe me. But in all honesty, we've never had a crime of that type in this county."

"Not yet," he said flatly.

Which was a point she couldn't argue. This county evidently always seemed peaceful until something blew up. It wasn't as frequent as in heavily populated areas, but it still happened.

The major was framed against the front windows,

the bright spring sunlight now casting him in silhouette. Not comfortable for her to look at.

She pointed to the metal chair beside her desk. "Sit,
please. I'm having trouble seeing you."

He came around immediately and sat. Now she had a
clear view of his face. It had the chiseled appearance of
someone in prime physical condition, and sun had put
some slight lines at the corners of his eyes. He looked
as unyielding as the concrete she suddenly imagined
him walking through. She suspected he wasn't going to
hang around just to identify Larry's body, which hadn't
yet come back from the medical examiner, and arrange
a funeral. No, he had other things on his mind.

"I'm not going to leave this town until the murderer
is caught."

"We'll find him," she said with more confidence
than she felt. So far they hadn't uncovered any clues.
At least none they could yet recognize. Maybe the ME
would find something.

"You find him, or I will."

Whoa. She felt her first stirrings of sympathy sliding away into apprehension. "Let us do our job. You *do*
realize that anything you find probably won't be usable
in court, because you won't have a warrant. You certainly don't want to get in our way or get yourself in
trouble with the law."

He didn't answer immediately. When at last he spoke,
his voice was clear, flat, hard. "I don't care what happens to me. This is about my brother. He deserves justice. The dead should get that. Justice. That's one of the
things Larry believed."

She saw pain pass over his face, quickly erased, and she sensed that this wasn't about his brother's death. Not exactly. Something else was going on here.

She also wondered what could be done about this man. He'd only said he wanted to find the murderer. He hadn't said he was going to do anything illegal in the process. What were they to do to prevent him? Jail him without a charge?

Never. So they were stuck with this cannon. Whether it was a loose one or not, she had no idea. She *did* suspect that a Ranger could probably cause more trouble than a typical man on the street.

"You need to talk to the sheriff," she said, ticking possibilities over in her mind. "If you coordinate your efforts with ours, there may be a way for you to satisfy yourself."

"Is he here?"

"He's at a county board meeting." To discuss funding for expanding the department by a couple more cops, hoping to get funding for a better dispatch situation. Sticking communications over in the corner with the coffee machines was becoming a problem. They needed better equipment, a place to put dispatch out of the line of fire and noise in the front office. She'd been kind of startled when she began working here to realize that the department had been so small for so long they were stacking most duties all in one room. Time to move into the twenty-first century.

But that didn't answer her immediate problem. She tried to lighten things a bit. "He said he'd be gone an hour nearly an hour ago. Given it's the supervisors and it's about money, it may become a longer wrangle."

His nod was short, sharp. The cold steel in his gaze hadn't lessened a bit. Okay, then...

"I'll wait."

She figured determination was bone-deep in this man. He had come here on a mission, one he considered righteous. Short of being given official orders, he wasn't going to be derailed. She hoped the sheriff would be able to find a way to steer him. From her position, there was little she could do or say without her boss's approval anyway.

"Larry," she said finally.

Those eyes became even sharper. "What about him?"

"I knew him. Only for the couple of months he was here, but we met in Mahoney's bar one night. He was enjoying a scotch, and I went in there to eat a ham sandwich, maybe have a beer. I sat at the bar near him, and we fell into conversation."

He waited.

"I liked him immediately. Nice man, but I probably wouldn't want to be the target of one of his investigative pieces."

The faintest of frowns flickered over the major's face. "No one would."

"Anyway, we hit it off. He told me he was a journalist and that he was here on sabbatical to write a book. He even laughed, saying every reporter had a book in their bottom desk drawer. He never said what he was writing about. Did he tell you why he came to the back of beyond?"

"No." His expression shut down again.

"I saw him a lot while he was here. He liked Mahoney's—said it was his nod to Hemingway, whatever that meant. Do you know?"

He shook his head. "Probably a literary reference. A few years ago, he joked to me that you couldn't drink your way into a novel."

She felt a smile ease the tension in her face. "Well, he wasn't trying to drink his way into anything. He appeared to like the atmosphere, even played darts with some of the regulars. Never a heavy drinker. We talked whenever we ran into each other, sometimes meeting at the diner for lunch. I've known a few reporters, and they're never wallflowers. He'd started making friends around here."

"That's Larry, all right."

She suspected this man didn't find it easy to make friends. But maybe she was wrong. Too soon to know, except that while she wouldn't like being the subject of Larry's investigation, she would hate being the subject of this man's ire.

"He started having card games at his place once a week," she went on. "He invited me, but I'm not into cards, so I didn't go. Maybe six or seven guys attended. Never any problem from our perspective. Which I suppose means they were reasonably quiet and didn't get disorderly. Not much of an analysis on my part." She tried another smile. "We're looking into those friends."

"Good."

"You never know what kind of resentments might

come out of a card game. Especially if they were gambling, but since Larry invited me, I doubt it."

"He was never a gambler that I know of. At least not that way. He gambled a whole lot in other ways."

Cat wondered if she'd just told him too much about the friends. About the card games. Dang, this man's mere presence was making her talk too much, maybe reveal too much. Everything about him demanded answers.

She had just decided to pick up some paperwork in order to truncate this conversation by comparing written reports to digital. Gage hated the duplicate work, both on computer and paper, but like it or not, the duplication was useful. Papers couldn't be manipulated as easily as a computer file, but a computer file was more readily accessible.

Just as she was probably about to mortally offend the major, the sheriff walked through the door.

"How'd it go, Sheriff?"

"High school wrestling match. Partial success." Gage Dalton was a tall man with a face scarred by burns. Long ago, when he was a DEA agent, he'd been the target of a car bomb. He still limped from his injuries, and even now some of his movements exhibited pain.

She spoke again before he could pass. Major Duke was already rising from his chair. Gage wasn't going to escape this, either.

"Sheriff, this is Major Daniel Duke, Larry Duke's brother. You need to speak with him."

Gage raised a brow on the unscarred side of his face. "Come with me, Major. My office is open."

The two men disappeared down the corridor, and Cat expelled a long breath, only just then realizing she'd been holding it. Tense. Lots of tension surrounded the major.

The dispatch desk crackled to life with a call. "Burglary at 1095 Elm Street. Need backup and forensics."

Cat wished she were able to answer the call. She had a strong feeling she wouldn't escape the major.

A HALF HOUR LATER, as she finished up comparing reports, Gage called from the hallway.

"Cat, could you come in here, please?"

Oh God, she thought. She glanced at the dispatcher, an elderly crone who smoked like a chimney under the No Smoking sign. She had learned quickly that Velma was a fixture who must be respected. A couple of deputies had told her that the only way Velma was going to leave her job was toes first. Cat had learned that Velma mothered them all.

"Good luck," Velma said in her smoke-roughened voice.

Apparently, Velma had gotten the same kind of impression from their visitor.

Cat squared her shoulders and marched back to Gage's office. Maybe, just maybe, he'd found a way to contain this man. It wouldn't help anything to have the major interfering with the investigation. He could jeopardize the case.

"Hey, Cat," Gage said when she reached his office. "Come on in, close the door and grab a seat."

Close the door? Gage almost never did that. She followed his request, sitting only a foot away from Daniel Duke. Who, she had to admit, was attractive. He would have been more so if she hadn't seen the subzero chill in his gaze.

She turned her attention to Gage, hoping he had a solution.

"It seems," he said, "that Major Duke is determined to assist our investigation."

Oh boy. Gage describing it as assistance probably didn't bode well.

"I can understand the major's concerns," Gage continued. "If he wants to talk to people around the county, I can't prevent him. There's nothing illicit in that. But I've also made it clear that he's going to have to stay within the law so he doesn't destroy any case against a murderer. I've also made it clear that we *will* enforce the law, so he'd better not interfere in any way with our investigation. He won't be helping if we have to arrest him."

Cat nodded, glad Gage had made those points. Unfortunately, she sensed there was a big *but* on the way. Worse, her presence in this room probably pointed to involving her in some capacity.

She couldn't zip her lips any longer. "Is Major Duke suggesting we can't do our job?"

She knew that wasn't it. This was a man who needed to take up his lance for the sake of his brother. He *needed* to be involved. Still, she wanted to make her disapproval clear.

"I don't think that's it," Gage answered. "He's just

not constitutionally capable of sitting on the sidelines, are you, Major?"

"No." A single syllable saying more than a page full of words.

"Anyway," Gage went on, "I can't prevent him from walking around asking questions or looking for some obvious clue that we need brought to our attention. Within the law, of course. So, we need to coordinate. You have a background in homicide investigations, Cat. You'll be our liaison, keeping me informed at all times. And, Major, if Deputy Jansen says we need a warrant for something, listen to her. We can get a warrant fast enough from Judge Carter if there's probable cause."

Oh man, Cat thought, feeling everything inside her become as taut as a guitar string. A brick wall and a concrete one had just met, and she couldn't tell which one of them had won. At least it appeared that Gage had gotten a few concessions.

But playing liaison on this? While she'd be glad of the change of pace, being more deeply involved with a murder investigation, she didn't want to do it this way. What was more, she'd known Larry, and that had been the primary reason she *wasn't* on the case. Why had Gage chosen her? Just because she had some experience?

She looked at Major Duke, fearing that trying to keep him in line would be like bull riding. Then she accepted the inevitable. This was her assignment, and even though it might put her on the wrong side of the investigation, in terms of her involvement, it was still important, and Gage thought it necessary. She had one burning question, however.

"How much information from our investigation should I share?"

"Whatever you deem necessary."

On her shoulders, then. Lovely.

GAGE HAD VELMA call another officer in to take over desk duty. "Seems like you two may need a bit of discussion. Get yourselves over to the diner for coffee, maybe lunch."

Cat smothered a sigh, figuring she was going to have to reinforce Gage's limits over coffee, and probably endure a brain picking by Major Duke.

They crossed the street together and walked halfway down the block to the City Diner, known to everyone as Maude's diner because of its cantankerous owner. Cantankerous or not, Maude was another of those people around here who was both a fixture and well loved. This kind of thing was also a part of the charm of living here.

For the first time, she faced the seated major across a table. She had a clear view in the light from the diner's front windows. Mavis, Maude's daughter, appeared in lieu of Maude but slammed down the coffee cups with similar disdain. She'd learned well.

They took their menus, and Cat remarked, "Everything is good, but everyone raves about the steak sandwich."

Cat ordered the chef salad. A light lunch seemed best when she didn't know how the conversation would go. Her stomach was already trying to knot. As she expected, Duke ordered the steak sandwich.

While they waited, he looked unflinchingly at her across the table. "You'd much rather volunteer to hike up and down Mount McKinley than be sitting here."

Actually, she would. She loved the mountains. "That obvious, huh?" Might as well be blunt, although she was bothered by being so readable. She'd tried for years to suppress that tendency in herself.

"I can't say I blame you."

Well, well. The admission surprised her. "Then you get it?"

"Yes." Their lunches arrived, and he sat back to allow the plates to be banged down in front of them. Coffee, dark and aromatic, filled their cups. She reached for one of the small creamers and dumped it in hers. Ordinarily she preferred her coffee black, but the way her stomach was feeling...

He glanced at his sandwich, then lifted half of it as though reluctant. He raised it partway to his mouth and looked at her over it. "I didn't ever not get it," he said before biting off a mouthful.

She paused with a container of blue cheese dressing hovering over her salad. "Then what was this all about?"

"Informing your office. Making a few things clear. Setting the boundaries I need to stay inside. Regardless, if you don't get the murderer, I *will*."

She believed him. She also feared what he might do if driven by rage. This man was trained to kill. "Then why do you want to know the boundaries? Isn't this a pointless exercise if you just want to shoot someone?"

"I might like to prevent this bastard from ever breathing again, but I'd prefer to see him locked up for life." He looked down a moment. "In my opinion, life in prison is a far worse sentence than a quick death."

She nodded, stabbing her fork into a swirl of chef's roll and salad. "I'd agree with that."

"But I'm not leaving here without finding him. I have three weeks."

"Now we've got a time limit?" She arched a brow.

"It's good to know the boundaries," he said, echoing himself and Gage's earlier remarks. "For both you and me."

She supposed it was. And now her favorite salad and dressing had become flavorless. It was then she faced needing to get a handle on herself. Most of what was going on was in her imagination. Maybe he hadn't pressed as many buttons as she'd thought. Maybe he wasn't here to rip up half the county in his search for his brother's killer. Maybe he didn't want to barge through this place like a furious bull.

It was time to find the common ground where they could work together. Because that was basically what Gage had handed her. A job that required finding that ground. With the major. She wondered how much of an eye she'd need to keep on him and if it was going to be full-time. She supposed she'd find out, but it would be a heck of a lot easier if she didn't start out in complete opposition.

He amazed her by saying, "I guess I didn't create a very good first impression with you."

"No. You didn't. You had death in your eyes."

"Hardly surprising," he retorted. He was already finishing the first half of his sandwich.

Cat had hardly made a dent in her lunch. She forced herself to take another bite before speaking. "Look, we've got to work together now. We need to find some mutual understanding."

"I thought the sheriff had made that clear."

"He set the rules. Repeatedly, if I know Gage. But this is about more than rules. You're going to have to work with me on this. I can't have you doing things and telling me about them later."

"Understood."

Oh really? she wondered.

"Let me make something clear, Deputy. I'm a military officer. I follow rules all the time, some of them quite restrictive. My own judgment generally comes into play only in combat and tactical operations where the situation is constantly shifting. I have to stay within the Uniform Code of Military Justice. On the other hand, when my superior tells me something like *Go take that hill*, I have to figure out how. There's a lot in the balance, not the least the safety of my soldiers."

"Okay," she answered, willing to listen.

"There's not really a conflict here."

Time would tell, she thought. At least now she could taste her salad. "How do you want to set this up?"

Which was giving him a lot of leeway. Still, she wanted to know how he envisioned what they were going to do together, then decide how much of it was possible. She could still try to be the rein on him. *Try* probably being the operative word.

He glanced away, ruminating as he finished his sandwich. "I want to get to know people who knew Larry. Try to figure out if they know anything or sensed anything. Sometimes people find it easier to talk to a grieving relative than a cop. Or am I wrong?" His gaze snapped back to her.

"I've been a cop since I started dealing with cases like this. I can't say for certain. One thing I *do* know is that friends and family try to avoid saying anything disparaging about the deceased." She almost winced as the word came out, knowing that it sounded cold. He was probably far from wanting to call his brother *deceased*.

"Never speak ill of the dead," he remarked. "Thing is, Larry wasn't perfect. Nobody is. Do I think it was impossible for him to have an enemy? Absolutely not. His job often made people furious at him. He could just as well have affected others around him the same way. I know he wasn't here long, but it doesn't always take long to make someone hate you. An ill-considered comment can be enough."

"Larry used words like a master."

"Exactly. And he could slice like a knife in very few words when he saw or heard something he didn't like. Anyway, people might find it easier to talk with me *because* I know Larry wasn't perfect. I hope."

That was a good point. Maybe. She ate another forkful of salad, getting a mouthful of delightful blue cheese, along with meat rolls. The knot in her stomach was easing, and her taste buds were evidently waking up.

He just wanted to speak to people who'd known his brother? Sounded innocuous enough. But there were other possibilities looming in the shadows. She stared down at her salad, suspecting that she'd let her tension leave too soon.

DANIEL DUKE STUDIED the woman with whom he'd been partnered. She clearly didn't like it any more than he did. He was a man used to going on missions and making his own decisions within the confines of what was legal. Things were different in a war, of course, but he knew where the bright lines were, and he kept himself within them.

He didn't like the idea of someone peering over his shoulder and trying to control him. She had been chosen to be his watchdog. He was already chafing at the idea. He could move more freely on his own.

The Ranger in him, he supposed. There had been a few times when he'd air-dropped into enemy territory with nothing to rely on but himself. He had always accomplished his mission.

He'd also seen enough of the expressions crossing Cat Jansen's face to guess that she didn't like this, either.

He'd managed to set her back up. In the long run, that wouldn't matter. He'd come here for two purposes only: to bury his brother and to find a killer. If the sheriff's people succeeded, he'd be content, although it wouldn't be as satisfying. But this wasn't about satisfying himself.

He glanced toward Cat as he finished his sandwich. It seemed she was eating without a whole lot of pleasure. Uncomfortable situation.

But he noticed again the arresting combination of

black hair and brilliant blue eyes, a combination that would make anyone look twice. It had been the first thing he had noticed about her when he walked through the door of the office. And while uniforms seldom enhanced a woman's attractions, he still felt hers from across the table. When she moved, he could tell that she was fit, maybe even athletic.

But he wasn't here to notice a woman's beauty or anything else. They needed to forge a working relationship somehow, although he'd have been satisfied to tell her to continue her other duties and he'd keep her informed.

She didn't strike him as the type who was going to give him a leash that long.

Oh hell, he thought and reached for a potato wedge. He'd begun all wrong, but he didn't know how he could have begun better. He was furious beyond words over his brother's murder. He wanted the killer to face trial at the very least, and when he returned to his battalion, he wanted to know the guy was in jail. Caught. Going up the river as fast as possible.

Only when justice lay within reach would he be able to properly grieve for Larry. Because justice had indeed been important to Larry, something he'd been willing to risk his neck over. Then there was Duke's own guilt. He'd never be able to overcome that now, but he could deal with finding justice. Finding peace for Larry.

He spoke at last, trying to discover a way to meet this woman somewhere in the middle. Neither of them was happy to be here.

"Larry always used to say that the dead can't rest without justice."

Her head lifted from her salad, and he felt again the impact of her eyes. "You said he believed in it."

"The thing is, my brother was a realist, hardheaded and fact oriented. Then he'd say something like that. It was one of the things that drove his reporting."

"While I only knew him a short time, I didn't see anything remotely fanciful in him." She paused. "So you think Larry won't rest?"

"I don't know what comes after we die. It's all a mystery, and I tend to rely on facts, too. But since I don't know, I want Larry to get his justice. And frankly, I want justice, too."

She nodded. "I understand."

She sounded as if she did. Well, maybe that was a step in the right direction. He certainly needed to find one, since he'd started wrong, at least as far as Cat was concerned.

Parsing through the problem, trying to come up with a strategy, he slowly ate potato wedges and gave Cat space to enjoy her salad while he looked out the window. Spring sunshine drenched the street, and all the buildings appeared to have arisen early in the last century. He suspected renovations in this town tried to preserve the past, not erase it.

Maybe she needed to understand that he hadn't *had* to come to the police. He'd done so because he didn't want to get in a war with the cops here. That could mess everything up. And while he'd tried to make that clear, he wasn't sure he had.

There was Cat's reaction. He had to figure out how to persuade her before this became a bigger problem.

NEARLY TWENTY MILES AWAY, in a fold in the earth that cradled them in secrecy, three men sat around a small fire. The stream that trickled beside them, clearly runoff from the remaining snow high above in the mountains, made a pleasant sound as the afternoon began to wane.

It was far nicer than many of the places where they'd made a surreptitious camp. They all dressed casually, like campers or hikers, in jeans and long-sleeved shirts of varying plaids. Hiking boots finished off the unimpressive ensembles.

"You getting anywhere?" asked Man One.

"I hate these new phones," Man Two remarked. He held a smartphone in his hand. "The only contacts I can find are in recent text messages. The rest must be in the cloud somewhere, and we can't even get cell coverage here."

"What's a cloud?" Man Three asked. "And how can you be sure those aren't his only contacts?"

"Oh hell," said the first man. "He was a reporter. He probably had hundreds of contacts."

"No help to us," said the third man. "Hundreds of contacts? How do we weed through that?"

"We look at only the ones around here," said Man Two. "But I need his cloud access, and he's got it protected. When he said he'd put a copy in a place we'd never find, he might have meant that. And breaking into the house of one of his poker buddies last night turned up zilch."

"Clouds aren't that safe," the first man said. "Remember when that motion picture company got hacked? He probably wanted a copy he could reach that would be safe. Maybe an external hard drive or flash drive."

"Or," said the second man, "he might have kept notebooks and files. You know, old-fashioned paper. I dated a reporter a few years ago. She always kept her notes on paper. In those reporter notebooks, for one, and she had drawers full of files."

The first man looked at him. "Any reason?"

"She said it was the best way to protect her sources. She said that too many people could get into her computer."

If a breeze hadn't been wending its way down the narrow gully, ruffling grasses and the just-grown leaves of spring, they might have heard a pin drop.

"Why didn't you mention this before?" the third man demanded. "We didn't know to look for that kind of stuff last night."

The second man shrugged. "Who thinks of paper files these days? I sure as hell don't. That just popped up from memory."

Their search had just gotten bigger.

"We can't break into that house again," said the second man.

"Nope," agreed the first man. "We may have screwed that up. But I'm still not sure about his poker buddies and other friends here. Did he know any of them well enough to turn over serious information to them? We don't know."

"There's no way to find out," said the second man.

"Maybe the most important thing we can do is find out *where* he stashed the information."

"There's another team working on his contacts back in Baltimore," the first man reminded him. "Maybe they'll find out."

"I hope so," said Man Three. "Because I sure as hell don't want to go back without finding something."

The three exchanged looks.

"Why," asked the second man, "do I feel like we're Curly, Larry and Moe?"

"Because," said the first man, "we weren't given decent intel. We have to do that as well as find the stuff."

They all fell silent again. Each of them was thinking of events in Afghanistan.

Then Man Three stirred. "Hey, One? Did you know Larry Duke?"

"Why?"

"Because when you were…interrogating him, I got the feeling you did."

"Never met him," came the clipped response from the first man.

The other two exchanged glances. Neither was quite sure they believed it. They knew they'd come for the money. What if Man One had a different agenda?

Chapter Two

Daniel Duke made his way to the town's only motel, the La-Z-Rest. It didn't take him long to recognize the place had probably been here since long before he was born, but it was clean. Compared to a lot of places he'd slept, he wouldn't have complained regardless.

He doffed his uniform, putting it into a garment bag and hanging it in the closet. The shirt went into a laundry bag the motel provided. He'd chosen to wear the uniform for his arrival because it acted like a credential all on its own. Now he shed it so he wouldn't stand out.

Then he pulled on regular clothes, jeans and a chambray shirt, pretty much what he wore at home. Blending in with the locals was something he'd needed to do at times during his career, and sometimes that blending had required clothes he wasn't used to wearing. This was easy by comparison.

He felt he'd gotten a reasonable first concession from the sheriff. He hadn't expected to take part in the official case, but he hadn't wanted to be totally hampered, either. He might have a minder in Cat, and yet as annoyed as she was with the situation—he couldn't blame her for that—she'd shown signs of coming down off her high horse.

Looking back over their initial meeting, in retrospect he saw that he had probably come across as critical of her department. He was a naturally blunt man because he needed things to be clear when managing his own troops. On the other hand, he knew how to play political games when required. Until recently he'd been on an accelerated path up the command ladder, probably destined for a star on his shoulder one day.

Not anymore.

The simmering anger over *that* tried to surge, but he battled it down. There was one thing and one thing only he wanted to focus on right now—finding Larry's killer.

All right, he'd been impolitic. He needed to find a way to correct that so he and Cat Jansen could jolt along. He'd walked in and talked to her like one of his troops, making it perfectly clear what he expected, both of her office and of himself.

He'd looked down instead of up. The sheriff was like his superior officer in these circumstances. That meant Cat was, too.

Ah, hell. Talk about getting off on the wrong foot.

Her face swam before his eyes, and he felt the whisper of attraction once again. She was pretty, all right, with delicate features and those amazing blue eyes.

He brushed that feeling aside, too. Wrong time. Worse, he suspected Cat would be furious if she suspected she'd aroused his interest for that reason.

Judging by the few things Gage had indicated about her during their conversation, Cat must be very competent as a law officer, and that was how she'd want to be evaluated. The only way. She hadn't worked hard to get here only to be treated like she was a woman first.

He'd seen enough of that problem since women had started completing the arduous Ranger training. They were surrounded by a sea of men, all too many of whom believed the Rangers were a man-only territory. Considering what those women could have done to any guy who got out of line, that had always struck Duke as a stupid attitude to have.

Those women were Rangers first. Cat was a law officer first.

That settled, he paced the motel room. He was a man used to being physically active, to training every day for the next assignment. He'd spent too much time bottled inside a plane and then a car. He needed to work out some kinks.

He did some push-ups, some crunches, some squats. They weren't enough. What he needed was a ten-mile run. Some of it uphill.

He'd brought workout clothes with him, but they'd been used primarily on station. Not the kind of thing to wear around here if he wanted a low profile.

Damn. He'd seen what looked like a department store on the other side of town on the main drag. He decided to walk there to stretch his legs and get some new clothes. It would give him some time to get the lay of the land.

He always wanted to know where he was, if there were any obstructions to escape, what the shortest routes were between points. Recon. Basic, simple recon. It would be a good use of his time, if not all his energy.

He'd feel more comfortable, too. This might not be a very dangerous place, but that wouldn't change the habits of most of his adult life.

WHEN CAT RETURNED to the office, hoping Gage might put her on the burglary case, the sheriff called her back to his office.

"Door?" she asked, resigned to an inquisition.

"Please."

For the second time that day, she closed it, then sat across the desk from him. "And the winner is…"

Gage flashed one of his crooked smiles. "How'd it go?"

"I suppose you mean with Major Duke."

He shook his head a bit. "So, are you being difficult?"

"I suppose I am. I don't know if you saw it, but the man who came through that door earlier had death in his eye. Cold. Furious. And more than capable of carrying out any threat."

Gage sighed, leaning forward to rest his forearms on his desk. His chair squeaked, and she guessed from his faint grimace that some part of him was objecting to the simple movement.

"He's a Ranger," Gage said. "And from what I know of them, which admittedly isn't a whole lot, he's been to war more than once, he's gone undercover in enemy territory and he might even have gone on a few solo missions. You don't get to be a major at his age unless you're being fast-tracked, and you need that kind of experience to rise in the officers' ranks if you're in special ops."

"All of which is to say you saw the look, too."

"It didn't surprise me. Add to that the fact he'd probably love to get his hands around the throat of the guy who killed his brother, and you've got a man who's exercising some serious restraint. Yeah, he's a pressure cooker right now."

"How comforting," she said dryly.

"Anyway, I don't expect you to be able to stop him if he gets set on something. I just want to know what he's doing. It may sound like babysitting, but it's not. You know the stakes."

Cat did indeed. She'd tried to make them clear to Duke herself, and she'd heard enough of what Gage had said to know he had as well.

"I guess he set my back up," she admitted.

"Can't imagine why." A bit of sarcasm crept into his voice. "Just keep in mind that he's a military officer. He's used to commanding and to taking charge. Neither of which we can have him safely doing, but as long as he knows you're watching, he'll control himself."

"He said he's used to staying within the lines."

"Another thing he's had to do to achieve his rank. Do I think he will? Most likely, unless fury overtakes him. No guarantees about that. Cat, I can't emphasize enough that he's been to war. Basically left civilization behind. Some of that always stays with you."

"I know." Springing to memory were a number of vets she'd had to deal with when they lost themselves in depression, alcohol and drugs, or when memory or ungovernable rage had taken over. War inflicted indelible scars. "Okay, I'll keep all that in mind. But I guess it tells me why the military have their own special bases."

Gage cracked a laugh. "Caged up, you mean?"

Cat finally relaxed enough to laugh, too. "That was unkind. Okay, I'll do the best I can, but I make no promises. I was thinking earlier that this is going to be like riding a bull."

"You ever done that?" Gage asked as she stood up.

"Hell, no. Do I look crazy?"

His laugh followed her as she walked down the hall.

Guy Redwing had assumed her position at the front desk. He looked bored. "Need a little excitement?" she asked him.

"Depends on what kind." He grinned. "I'm starting to think about a beer at Mahoney's after work. Come with?"

She'd have liked to go with him, but before the words slipped out, she remembered she had a task with no punch-out time. And just then she saw Major Duke striding purposefully down the street. Hadn't he gone to the motel?

Wondering what he was up to, she said, "Sorry, Guy. Much as I'd like to, I just saw my current assignment walking down the street. Later."

She darted out the door and saw Major Duke looking across the street at Freitag's Mercantile. She quickened her pace, wanting to catch up. He must have heard her footfalls, because he turned swiftly. The speed of a striking cobra. Okay, this man was wired.

When he saw her, he relaxed and waited, so she adopted

a more reasonable pace. She didn't want any passersby to think she was chasing the man. Even if she was.

She nodded and smiled at the greetings from other residents who appeared to be on errands. One woman in particular was trying to wrangle twin boys, who were just of an age to slip her grip and make her look harried.

"Hi, Joan," she said as she passed.

"Hi, Cat. Boys!" She dashed off after them.

Cat was grinning by the time she reached Duke. "That's a handful."

"Those boys? Plenty of energy."

Then she faced him. "Looking for something?"

"Workout clothes that aren't stamped with Army logos all over. This is the place, right?"

She nodded. "Old-timey, with creaky wooden floors that have probably been there for at least a century. However, now that we have an influx of students at the community college, you'll find all the latest and greatest in some items. You want superhero shorts? I think they have some."

He surprised her with a short chuckle. "I don't think I'm ready to go that far. So are you my armed escort now?"

To her horror, she felt her cheeks heat. How had he done that? It had been a long time since she'd blushed. "I'm kinda over-the-top, huh?"

"No, you're in uniform, is all. Are you planning to join me in the store? Or later after I change and go for a run around town? You might find it hard in that utility belt."

Her cheeks grew even warmer. "Point taken."

He shook his head slightly. "How were you supposed to know what I was doing? This is going to be impossible for both of us if you have to be the principal and me the student reporting my every activity. Tell you what. I'll let you know if I'm doing anything that approaches the case. Then you can relax and I can go running."

Her cheeks didn't cool any, but she *was* just trying to do this job. An unfamiliar job. New rules and groundwork were needed. On the other hand, he was lengthening his leash and asking her to trust him. Having known his brother, she was inclined to, but the simple fact was that Major Duke was a stranger to her. Plus, she'd seen the icy fury in his eyes. He wasn't going to make this easy for either of them.

"I understand your point, Major."

"Duke. Just call me Duke."

"Okay, Duke. You can call me Cat. But you were walking down the street a few hours after having expressed your intention to interview people who knew Larry while he was here." As she mentally reviewed what he'd said when she'd first reached him, she started to get seriously irritated. How dare he talk to her that way? He'd scolded her as if she were a thoughtless kid.

He nodded slowly, glanced across the street and said, "Give me your cell number. I promise to tell you before I talk to anyone, okay?"

"Or anything else to do with your brother's murder."

"On my honor."

She relaxed a bit. She suspected honor was very important to this man. "All right. I'll trust you. But if I find you've crossed the line, you're going to be in trouble. I won't stand for it, nor will the sheriff."

"We'll get it sorted. Your number?"

"I want yours, too."

"Of course."

"Keep in mind, though, the farther you get out of town, the spottier cell reception will be. Out there in the ranch land, there aren't a whole lot of cell towers. Not enough people to justify them. And the mountains are pretty much the same."

"I've operated in much tougher conditions."

Yeah, he had, she thought as she walked back to the office after they'd exchanged numbers. That was part of what worried her.

CAT WAS A FIREBRAND, Duke thought as he crossed to the mercantile. He had no doubt she'd try to call him to heel if she didn't like something. He'd only promised to let her know what he was up to, but she'd have to give him reasons if he objected.

While he was looking at shorts, a memory of Larry popped up. They'd often run together while they were growing up, but when Duke had returned from Ranger training, Larry had wanted to run with him again. The two of them had wound up laughing because Larry could no longer keep up the distances or the pace Duke used. He'd never forgotten his brother's grin as he asked, "What did they do? Replace you with bionics?"

God, he missed his brother, even though they'd been estranged for a while. Which made him ponder yet again how he—or anyone else, for that matter—

allowed such rifts to grow when life was so short. You never knew...

He should have learned that after so much time in deadly environments. Life could often be too short, truncated by unexpected events.

Shaking himself out of impending gloom, he focused instead on rage. He'd have time to grieve later, once Larry had his justice.

He found a couple of pairs of shorts and some shirts and walked back to the motel. Man, he needed to run. A long, fast run.

Then he'd figure out what to do next.

WELL, THAT HAD gone well, Cat thought as she walked back to the office. *Not.* He'd managed to embarrass her, which wasn't easy in her line of work. Or maybe anger had heated her cheeks, not embarrassment. Regardless, after that she could easily dislike him.

It wouldn't help anything to dislike him, though. Not one thing. Besides, she could understand his thirst to find his brother's killer. She'd known more than one family who had been pursuing justice for a dead relative decades after the killing. Not unusual. Some called it closure, some referred to it as justice, but there was no escaping the fact that people needed a resolution. That need could consume them, and possibly their lives.

Cops understood that. They understood it so well that departments with sufficient resources ran a cold case unit. No one wanted to forget the dead.

A few cops even investigated cold cases after they retired, so haunted were they by some crimes.

So yeah, she got it. Totally. Which meant she needed to quell her reactions to Duke. They were too strong. Too reactive. She'd dealt with worse than a difficult relative before.

And that was what he was. However intimidating, however angry, he was still a grieving brother who needed his resolution.

Needing it in three weeks was the only unreasonable part. Larry hadn't been here long enough to create a big list of persons of interest. A poker group, eight people max? Not much to go on.

Nor were the regulars he'd met at Mahoney's, although they wouldn't be overlooked as the department worked to peel back the layers on this case. If there'd been an argument or altercation, Mahoney would know. If it had been bad enough, he'd have reported it. Nothing had seeped out of that bar.

When she returned to a desk she shared with other officers, she realized she was at loose ends. Her assignment to keep an eye on the major made it impractical to follow any kind of duty that she couldn't quit immediately.

Damn it. She *liked* to work. In fact, she liked it so much she averaged about sixty hours a week. That curtailed her social life, but that was okay. She was an introvert in an extrovert's job. Interacting with people all day made her crave solitude with a book or a movie. Recharging.

Or maybe she could work out in her tiny gym in her basement. The house her mother had left her on Poplar had made it possible, which was good because this town had one gym open to the public: at the college. Public hours were limited, of course, making its use more difficult.

The house was cozy, which suited her. Just two bedrooms and a dine-in kitchen, no dining room. One full bath. The extra bedroom served as her home office and contained the daybed she'd slept in while caring for her mother.

It was a newer house than many neighboring ones that had been built during the waning days of the Victorian era, but it displayed nice touches with dark woodwork and matching solid-core oak doors. Over the time since her mother's death, she'd started repainting the interior and had indulged her love of color, such as the Wedgwood blue in the living room and sunshine yellow in the kitchen.

When she walked through the door, she initially felt sorrow. Despite having many good memories here, she also had a lot of sad ones, and every time she entered the house, she missed hearing her mom call out, *Hi, honey.*

Sometimes she was almost sure she'd heard the greeting. Each time it happened, it arrested her. Even in midstep, she'd pause, listening.

She changed quickly into her workout clothes and headed down into the basement. There her weights, her exercise bike and her treadmill awaited her. This wasn't her favorite part of the house, but it was a necessary one, holding the washer and dryer, a utility sink and various boxes of stored items.

Items that she kept thinking she should give away.

She had no use for her mother's clothes, for one thing. She'd already saved what she cared about.

An hour later, wishing for a TV so she'd have something other than her own rambling thoughts to keep her company while she exercised, she took her sweat-soaked body upstairs for a shower.

Then it was time to consider dinner. Dang, her life outside of her job had become a totally predictable routine. Exercise, dinner, book or DVD, or sometimes some browsing on the internet.

Occasionally she wondered if that was a reaction to all the many months she'd spent looking after her mother. A time to heal, maybe a time to hide from personal cares.

Whatever. She was in no mood to do anything about it just then. Major Daniel Duke was probably going to invade her entire life with his quest. He'd taken over the job part of it. Now she could live in expectation of getting a phone call even at night as he told her what harebrained thing he was planning to do.

She caught herself. "Not fair," she said aloud to the empty house. She had to stop ascribing things to him she couldn't yet know.

He'd really set her back up, right from the time he'd first walked into the office.

Why?

When it came, the answer annoyed her no end. He was attractive. Very attractive. A trickle of warmth passed through her as she visualized him. *Oh yeah.*

She needed that like a hole in her head.

Chapter Three

Duke decided to get breakfast at the truck stop diner across the highway from the motel. The rain outside was steady, and while it wasn't a downpour, there was more of it than a drizzle. The air felt a bit chilly as he stepped outside, making him glad of his lightweight jacket. Georgia had warmer weather, and he seemed to have lost the cold conditioning from Afghanistan. A few more days and he'd adapt.

If there was one thing he was confident of, it was his ability to adjust even to the worst conditions, and this was a long way from bad.

With a clearer head, he grew dubious about what he was doing here. As he ate a large breakfast, he wondered what he hoped to accomplish. Yes, he wanted justice for Larry. Yes, he wanted the killer behind bars on a murder charge. Yes, he'd been furious and aching with grief since he got the news.

But what was he going to do?

It wasn't as if he had a list of Larry's contacts here. As he'd been running the streets of this pleasant town late yesterday, he'd calmed down a bit and really looked around. No matter what he did, he was going to be a visible stranger in these parts.

Why should anyone talk to him? Maybe a few of Larry's acquaintances here might, but how was he to find them? Larry was a meticulous note taker, so maybe he had some contacts at his home. Or maybe the cops had them.

Damn.

As he ate, gloom crept up again. He needed to fight for Larry, but he'd been stupid. His mission strategy had been essentially zip. Get out here and talk to people. Right. What people?

Maybe he could get Cat to give him some names, but considering the resistance he'd felt in her yesterday, he wasn't hopeful. Naturally she resented him thundering onto her turf. How would he have felt if she'd shown up at Fort Benning and made demands of him?

He'd have resisted, too.

He stared down at his plate, still holding eggs, bacon and home fries that he no longer wanted to eat. He forced himself to chew and swallow. A soldier learned to eat whenever the opportunity showed up, and he loathed wasting food anyway. He'd seen too many people who didn't have enough to fill their bellies.

So what now, genius? he asked himself.

Yesterday when he'd been running, he'd imagined Larry on these same streets. It had proved hard to do. Larry was a big-city guy, associated for much of his career with major daily newspapers. He thrived on the action both in his work and in his environment. He collected interesting stories from many he met, just because he was that kind of guy, truly interested in other people.

He remembered Larry saying once, "Everybody has a story, Dan. Most of them are fascinating."

Larry had lived as hard as he had worked, fearless and daring. This town just didn't seem like him at all. At least from what Duke had seen.

Which wasn't much. He faced it—he was going into this mission mostly blind. It couldn't be helped by learning a language, adopting local dress and eating local food so he wouldn't smell different to people.

It was vastly more complicated. He was out of place, and people around here would figure that out. They'd be rightfully suspicious about him hanging around, and not even the excuse of preparing a funeral or a burial would give him enough cover. Definitely not if he started asking questions.

Nor was three weeks necessarily long enough to solve a case.

Anger and frustration goaded him anew. He *had* to do more than that. Larry deserved more than being boxed and put in the ground.

And nothing, but nothing, could make up for their estrangement. They'd both had a part in it, but Duke had still been simmering when he got the news about Larry. Still unable to find his way back. Hell, they had been two brothers locked in separate notions of what had been right.

He pushed that away, too. It would do no good now.

Outside the rain continued to fall.

CAT STARTED TO get uneasy when the morning passed without Duke showing up or her phone ringing. Was he out attempting some kind of investigation without telling her? She hated to think she'd have to rely on people around here telling her what he was doing.

And tell her they would. Or tell any deputy. He was an unknown man from unknown parts, and they'd gossip. Or if he made anyone uneasy, they'd call or walk in the office door.

Whatever he was doing, nobody found it remarkable enough to pass it along to the office.

Thank goodness.

Twice she pulled out her cell to call him but changed her mind. After yesterday, she didn't want to seem ridiculous. There had to be some trust on her part, or he might decide he was done with her and the whole department.

But she remained uneasy. Finally, she decided that if he didn't call her by noon, she would call him.

Satisfied, she made some busywork for herself at the office, all the while yearning to go back to regular duty. She couldn't even go complain to Gage about this impossible task, because he hadn't come in yet. Probably out talking to someone.

Not that she would complain. Nope, she prided herself on not being the type.

Shortly before noon, she could barely rein her impatience, but then Duke walked through the door. She summoned a smile, opening her mouth to speak.

He forestalled her. "I was over at the mortuary. They don't have any release date for Larry's body."

"The state has him," she answered. "We don't have the kind of forensics here that they have."

His eyes narrowed, but he didn't say more than "Can we get coffee?"

She grabbed her yellow uniform rain jacket. "We can go to Maude's if you don't mind a lunch crowd. Or we can go to Melinda's Bakery. She has a handful of tables for people who want to enjoy coffee and pastry, although at this time of day she's probably nearly sold out of baked goods."

Remarkably, he hesitated. While she'd known him less than a day and her experience of him was literally a couple of hours, he didn't strike her as indecisive.

"Or," she said reluctantly, "we can go to my place, where no one might overhear."

He raised an eyebrow. "Very generous."

"Well, I don't know what you want to discuss. You decide how much privacy you need."

"I don't want to impose."

Which was probably as good as saying he didn't want the diner or the bakery for this discussion.

"My place it is," she answered. "You got a car?"

"I walked here from the motel."

"Can't cage the beast, huh?"

A flicker of humor appeared then was gone. "Nope."

"Let's go."

The distance to her house wasn't that great, but given it was raining, she didn't feel like walking it as she often did. Plus, the sooner they got to her house, the sooner they could get this conversation underway and she could stop wondering if he was about to lob a bomb.

The drive was short enough but worth it just to watch him fold his way into her subcompact. She almost grinned, but he succeeded.

Once at her house, she started a pot of coffee and invited him to sit at her small kitchen table. There was room for a larger table, but it was the one her mother had used for many years, and it was enough for her.

He sat on one of the chairs that had a steel frame

and a vinyl-covered seat. A relic of the '50s or '60s, she believed.

While the drip coffee maker hissed and gurgled, she sat facing him. "What's up?"

"Well, there's my brother. I get he was murdered, but what's taking so long?"

"All I can say is that it shouldn't be much longer. I don't know the timetable. I'm not sure anyone in the office does, but I'll ask."

"Thanks." He pushed the chair back so he could cross his legs, ankle on knee. "I have another question. I'd like to see where my brother was living. Have you people released it yet?"

"Hoping to find some information?"

"It's possible."

God, she didn't want to say this, but she was going to have to because there'd be no other way. "It may have been. But… Duke? Are you sure you want to see it? Nothing's been cleaned up. You should hire someone…"

He shook his head. "I've seen worse."

She frowned. Her heart skipped unhappily. "You may have seen worse, Duke, but worse wasn't your brother."

THE WORDS HIT Duke hard. He felt his own head jerk a little in shock. He was getting warned about something far worse than he'd imagined. Shot? He'd seen plenty of gunshot victims. She had to know that, so what was she warning him about?

And she was right. Before this, it hadn't been his brother.

"What aren't you telling me?" he asked quietly. "What are you concealing?"

He watched her look away briefly. Then slowly her

gaze returned to him. "It was ugly. I can't provide any details until we get the full report, but there's a reason we didn't give it to our local coroner. Can we just leave it at that for now?"

Black rage filled him, a rage so black that for a little while he didn't see Cat or the room around him. His hands clenched as if he could wrap them around someone's throat. God, he wanted to. Badly.

He closed his eyes, forcing the fury down into an internal box he'd had to use many times. It contained all the seething dark things inside him, the only place he could store them.

"I see."

"Do you?" she asked.

"Unfortunately, I do."

She compressed her lips, then opened them to speak. "Most people don't go back to where a tragedy like this happened. They stay away until cleaners come in to deal with it. There are some things people don't want seared into their minds."

"I get it." He certainly did. "But I've seen it all, I think."

"You probably have. But *not when it's your brother.*" She spoke emphatically.

The anger threatened to escape his control once again, but it wouldn't be fair to level it at this woman. She was doing her job as best she could. As for Larry... it was true, he didn't want to see it, but he didn't know how he could avoid it.

He drew a long breath, then said, "You don't want me to see it because you're afraid of what I might conclude. What I might see with experienced eyes."

A spark flared in her blue eyes. "Eyes experienced with a battlefield, not with a crime. You might draw the wrong notions about things. I've seen a lot, too, Duke, and I wouldn't reach conclusions until we get the forensics report."

As his anger settled back into the dark box, he admitted she had a point. He didn't have to like it, but she had one.

"What about Larry's contacts?" he asked. "I assume you know who they are. That you pulled every bit of information out of his place that you thought might be useful. You can tell me about that."

Her blue eyes sharpened as they studied him, making him feel almost like a bug under a microscope. Then she rose, pulled a couple of mugs out of the cupboard and poured coffee. "You like it black?"

"Yes."

He was still waiting, wondering if she was going to stonewall him. He watched her return with the mugs and sit down. He reached for his and cradled it in both hands. Hot. It was hot, and his fingers were not.

Eventually she spoke. "I'm going to give you one name. He'll tell you what he chooses. He's not a suspect, because he was out of town during the time frame of the murder."

He forgot everything else. "Who?"

"Ben Williams. Larry's boyfriend."

CAT WATCHED SHOCK hit him again. She leaned forward at once, a new conviction growing.

"You know him?"

"I don't know." He shook his head and put his mug down on the table. "I served with a Ben Williams. He left the Army a couple of months or so before…"

He stopped.

"Before what?"

"It's not relevant. Thing is, I introduced a Ben Williams to Larry one night about four years ago when we were all at a bar. They hit it off. Then Ben resigned his commission sometime later and I never saw him or heard about him again. It can't be the same man."

"Maybe not. I wouldn't know. I do know Ben moved here more than two years ago."

"That could be him. But why here?"

"I seem to remember he grew up here." She was trying to digest the possible ramifications if this was the same man. "Larry and Ben were quiet about their connection, though. I don't think many people even guessed they were an item. Ben never went to the card games, and I'm not aware of the two of them hanging out in public."

"Then how'd you find out?"

"Because Larry told me in passing, then asked me to sit on it. I'm not sure if it was one beer too many or if he just needed to tell someone. I had to share it when Larry died, obviously."

"Of course."

She could sense him thinking and she was doing the same. If Ben was the same guy Duke knew, and Ben and Larry had known each other long ago... Well, what did it mean?

She spoke again, sorting through what she knew. "Ben was in Gunnison visiting friends for a week at the time. When I called him, he dropped everything to get back here. We can go talk to him if he's willing."

Duke nodded. His gaze had grown distant, as if he were searching his own memory. "I don't know if my Ben Williams was gay. But if he was, military life must have been damn near unendurable. The changes in policy didn't change much on the ground. Some things can only become hidden, but never change."

She sat for a few minutes, sipping coffee, absorbing what he'd said. Eventually she asked, "Is it widespread?"

"The bigotry? I can't quantify it. One thing I know is that peer pressure is strong, and in a military unit more so. You live and die by the people you serve with, and sometimes it takes only one bad apple to affect everyone. It doesn't help when the command structure flips back and forth on gays in the military."

Duke sighed. "Anyway, a lot of those bad attitudes disappear under fire. Some people quickly realize that all that matters is whether you can trust the soldier beside you to have your back." He offered her a half smile. "Incoming fire can change your perspective on a lot of things. Or not."

Cat tried to imagine what it must be like for a commanding officer—at least she assumed Duke was at his rank—to have to deal with so many different problems. Not just how to fight and when to fight. Not just the stuff that sprang to mind when she thought about the Army.

"You have a lot on your plate."

"All I can do is be thankful for NCOs. They handle most of the nitty-gritty. Still, we're dealing with a lot of very young men. More hormones than brains, I sometimes think, but that's part of what makes them damn fine soldiers."

She laughed quietly. "You were that age once."

"Yeah, I was. I remember and shake my head at some

of the crazy things I did." Then he zeroed in on his main concern. Not an easy man to divert. "Can we call Ben?"

She hadn't expected him to drop it, but she'd been hoping to avoid it for a while. She'd have liked to speak to Ben first and tell him Duke wanted to meet him. That would give Ben a chance to refuse, and he should have it. Ben had to be drowning in his own grief.

Allowing her a private conversation wasn't going to work with this man. On the other hand, she could see why. Was Duke supposed to trust *her* not to tell Ben to keep silent?

Cat twisted a little and pulled her cell phone out of her pocket. She kept related phone numbers on her contacts list while a case was ongoing and removed them later. Ben was there.

He answered on the third ring. Cat immediately identified herself.

Ben said almost eagerly, "What have you found out?"

"We're still looking for more evidence. I called because I need to ask you something."

"I told you I was out of town. Didn't you verify that?"

"That's not what I'm calling about, Ben, but yes, we verified your alibi."

A bitter laugh came over the phone. "Yeah. My alibi. That sounds so good, doesn't it?"

"It's a criminal investigation," she reminded him, trying to keep her tone kind. He was going through hell.

Ben's impatience came through. "Just find the killer. So what did you want?"

"Larry's brother would like to talk to you. Major Daniel Duke."

"I know who he is." Ben fell silent, the quiet conveying his reluctance. "Yeah. Okay. Why not?"

"You don't have to."

"Then you don't know Duke."

Cat was beginning to know him. She understood Ben perfectly.

Ben spoke after another hesitation. "Look, I don't know what I can tell him. I don't know what Larry was working on. He never, not once, talked about it. That was the toughest part about caring for him. He gave new meaning to the word *secrets*."

But Cat felt her heart thunder. "You think his murder had something to do with his work?" She wasn't sure anyone had considered that possibility. Larry had been here writing a book. Had his work followed him all the way from Baltimore?

"I don't know what else it could be. It sure as hell wasn't your ordinary burglary. But yeah, I'll talk to Duke. Where and when?"

"Privacy?" Cat asked.

Ben sighed. "That would be good, I guess. Bring him out here. I'll put the coffee on."

"Thanks, Ben. See you in a bit."

After she disconnected, she looked at Duke. "Let's mount up. He'll see you now."

Ten minutes later they drove through the rain toward Ben's house, an older structure on what could be called a mini ranch. In the past, a piece of a much larger ranch had been carved out for one two-story house surrounded by about forty acres. Cat suspected the subdivision had occurred for the benefit of one of a rancher's children. She couldn't imagine why else that could have happened.

Maybe one of these days she ought to go to the library and talk to the librarian. Miss Emma, as everyone called her, was reputed to be a truly great resource when it came to county history. Her family had been among the first to settle here in the late nineteenth century. Her father had also been a judge here.

Someday, she promised herself.

Beside her, Duke said nothing. Either he was lost in his own thoughts or he just didn't speak idly.

That might be difficult to get used to. No casual chitchat? She wasn't accustomed to people who could remain silent for long. On the other hand, she admitted she wasn't much for it herself.

A half hour brought them to Ben's house, set back a few hundred yards from the county road. Tall evergreens towered along the property line, a useful windbreak.

Ben, a slender man wearing jeans and a gray sweatshirt, met them on the porch. His face, ordinarily attractive, now looked gaunt. To judge by the dark circles around his eyes, he hadn't been sleeping well.

Cat discovered that no introduction was needed. Ben was apparently the same guy Duke had known. Neither of them seemed especially warm in their brief greeting.

The old kitchen was a large room, big enough for a long table that could easily seat a big family or some ranch hands. It must have come with the house, since it was larger than a size most people would have purchased nowadays. Ben seemed awfully alone there.

He waved them to the table, grabbed three mugs in one hand and the coffeepot in the other.

He poured for all of them before sitting across the table. "What's this about, Duke?"

"Trying to get a picture. I want Larry's murderer."

"Don't we all?" Ben's laugh was bitter. "You care now?"

"I always cared."

Ben looked away briefly. "I suppose."

"I was wrong," Duke said flatly. "He wasn't exactly innocent, either. But you always think there'll be a tomorrow."

"Yeah. Only tomorrow disappeared."

Cat watched them both, wishing one or the other would fill in the blanks, but refusing to ask them. She had to let this roll between the two men, at least for now. The tension between them was almost palpable.

"Look," Duke said, "I'm sure I don't have to tell you about Larry's thirst for justice. I can't do anything else now except try to make sure he gets it."

Ben passed a hand over his face, and when he dropped it, there was a sheen in his eyes, as if he were fighting back tears.

"It made him a great investigative reporter," Ben said tautly. "You should know that."

"I *do* know," Duke replied. "I know it all the way to my gut."

"Then why did you freeze him out?"

Duke shook his head. "We froze each other out. I was angry because Larry didn't give me a heads-up on that story about the murders. I kept hoping that the repercussions would die down, but after my next performance report, I realized that story killed my career. If I'd known it was coming, I might have been able to distance myself."

Ben looked down. "He was right."

"About what? The crimes? Of course he was. But when his piece hit the papers, I couldn't begin to do damage control. I was suspected of being his source, when I hadn't known a thing about it until Larry's story was smeared all over the papers. Maybe you were suspected, too. I don't know."

"I wouldn't have cared!"

"Maybe you wouldn't, but you were already terminating. I wasn't. I was damned with faint praise, and there went any hope I had of promotion. I'm still getting damned."

Ben half smiled, but it contained no mirth. "No stars for you."

"Worse, no light colonel. I'm done at twenty."

It almost seemed they were speaking in code. Cat knew she'd have to ask for some explanations later, but right now she let the men talk.

Ben retorted, "Larry wanted justice for those victims. He wanted to see the perpetrators punished. Your motivations were selfish."

"Maybe. Maybe not. All I know is I felt betrayed by my brother."

Ben swore quietly. "He couldn't tell anyone about that story before it hit the presses. Those higher up the food chain would have done everything they could to squash it."

Duke didn't answer. Cat wondered if it was because he agreed with what Ben had just said, or if there was another reason. She hoped her growing list of questions would stick with her. She wished she could write them down, but she didn't want to do anything that might halt this conversation.

Eventually it was Duke who broke the silence. "What was he working on while he was here?"

"I don't know. Larry was always secretive. I have no

idea whether that was to protect the people who gave him information, or if it was for other reasons."

"Secrets caused us to split," Duke answered. "Given that story, I've got to wonder if he was working on something new that worried someone."

"I've wondered, too," Ben admitted. "I thought that once he arrived here, we'd be able to be more open about our relationship. No. Larry urged me to keep it quiet."

"Maybe he thought he was protecting you."

"And maybe he thought the same thing about you. Did you consider that? Why would he think you'd be connected to his reporting in any way?"

"He didn't know the Army," Duke answered. "I'll grant him that in retrospect."

Ben looked as if he might have eaten something sour. "I do know the military. I understand. God knows I faced enough of it."

Once again Duke shook his head. "I never heard a word about your sexual orientation."

"A lot of people had figured it out. Enough so that I wasn't surprised when my performance reports started going downhill."

"You, too? I was never in your chain of command, so I didn't see them."

For the first time these men shared a look of understanding.

After a minute, Ben spoke again. "It's a great way to hide prejudice, saying someone is excellent but not rating him or her higher."

Cat interjected a question, feeling it might be safe. "Better than excellent?"

"Oh yeah," Duke answered. "*Stands out above all peers* in the written comments is a good one."

"Oh man," she murmured.

"Lots of little, ugly secrets," Ben remarked. "You can make someone's life hell without ever revealing something that might be against regulation. You know, like discrimination that policy doesn't allow."

She was getting a much clearer idea of what Larry's story might have done to Duke, and why he might have stopped speaking to his brother. Other details she would ask about later, like the thrust of the story. It could be relevant.

Ben was relaxing a little. Duke seemed to be as well. Evidently they'd gotten past the problem between the brothers. At least for now.

"What are you looking for, Duke?" Ben asked. "My absolution?"

"No. Every single day I'm going to regret that I didn't try to close the gap between us. Too late for that. I'm hoping you might know something, anything, that could help to find his murderer."

Ben lifted his hands almost helplessly. "I told the sheriff everything I could think of, and there's little enough. I'm sure he had enemies from his reporting. I *do* know that he received threats, some of them death threats. But that was all back East. I don't think he ever got one here. If he did, he never said a word."

The rain grew heavier. For the first time, Cat heard it rattling like pellets against the kitchen window. Ben looked around, noticing.

Duke spoke. The man could not be deterred. "Why did he come out here to write a book?"

Ben smiled sadly. "I thought he came for me."

"I wouldn't be surprised," Duke answered. For a few more minutes, he appeared to be looking at something far away. "Larry didn't ask for a lot. Just to tell a good story and to have his own family. I guess you gave him that, Ben. Thanks."

Ben nodded, his face sagging once again.

Duke rose then pulled out his cell. "Let me text you so you'll have my number. If you think of anything…"

"I doubt I will. But if I do, I'll call Cat."

Cat was surprised that Duke didn't bridle. He'd just been effectively dismissed by Ben.

But Duke did no such thing. "Let me know if you need anything. I'll help however I can."

THE RAIN WAS still coming down heavily, the distant sky and land meeting in an impenetrable gray. Driving them back to town, Cat tried not to drum her fingers impatiently on the steering wheel. She had so many questions.

But Duke remained mute beside her until she finally asked, "Are you going to run in this weather?"

"It wouldn't be the first time."

"I'm sure, but the question stands."

"The answer is probably."

"Well, I want to talk with you, so fit me in."

At that he turned his head. She glanced his way then returned her attention to the road. Too dangerous to get distracted.

"Pick a time," she continued. Getting pushy with this guy seemed like the best route.

"As soon as we get back. I'd like a drink."

An interesting non sequitur. She wondered if he felt a need after that conversation with Ben. "What do you want? I don't keep anything strong at my house, but I've got a few bottles of beer. Or we could go to Mahoney's bar. It probably isn't busy at this hour, and they do make a good sandwich. In fact, I'm getting very hungry."

"It's late afternoon already." He sounded surprised.

"Yup." Not much else she could say.

More silence. The rain fell heavily enough that water couldn't run off the road fast enough. She slowed even more and waited.

"Any place we can get takeout?"

"Of three places, two of them do it. Well, the market also sells subs. Depends on what your preference is."

"You're the one who's hungry. Me, I eat whenever I can, whatever I can."

Cat decided instantly. "Then it's a sub. I'm starved, and a loaded one just might do it for me."

The rain let up just as they reached the edge of town. The city looked sad in the gray light and rain. It suited her mood perfectly.

The market deli was quick, making the eight-inch subs in a relatively short time. Duke ordered an extra one and insisted on paying.

Cat greeted some of the other customers. Part of the job, although she didn't mind the casual hellos. People around here rarely ignored someone they knew, and much of the time when you passed somebody in a vehicle, fingers would lift while the palm remained on the steering wheel. A friendly gesture that had almost faded in a lot of places she'd been.

Back at her house, she didn't bother with plates. They could eat off the wrappers with the assistance of a couple of napkins. Her only effort was to get two bottles of beer out of her fridge and put them on the table.

Duke pulled the tops off both. My, she thought,

wasn't this cozy? Hardly. He looked grim, and she braced herself.

"What was going on back there?" she asked, unable to bury her questions any longer. "It was like the two of you were speaking in code some of the time."

"It probably sounded that way. I don't know which part of it I want to discuss right now."

"You want me to ask questions? Or wait until after you've eaten."

By then he was chewing on a large bite of his sandwich. She joined him as her hunger won over her curiosity. Food first, she decided. She had him temporarily corralled, and everything else could wait. Why ruin good food with heavy emotion?

"You know," she said presently as food settled into her stomach and quieted the gnawing hunger, "I've got a treadmill in my basement. Some weights, too. If you'd rather do that than run in this rain, I'll share."

"Thanks. I might take you up on that."

"No barbells, though. It would be too dangerous when I'm alone. But I do have a curling bar."

He nodded, then gave her a faint smile. "Got any additional weights for those dumbbells?"

"Oh yeah, iron plates. Can't make it with those pretty little ones that come in different weights."

"Sounds good to me."

Given his career, he was probably an exercise demon. She almost looked forward to watching him wrestle those plates around.

When he finished his first sandwich, he offered her half of the second, but she shook her head. "I'm full, thanks."

The beer went down smoothly, icy cold and tangy. Then she was done eating, and he was close to it.

"What happened back there?" she asked. "At Ben's." As if he needed the elucidation.

"I think Ben and I came to an understanding. At least as far as Larry is concerned. Kind of feeling our way there."

"What happened between you and Larry?"

His face darkened, and she wasn't sure he was going to tell her anything. She was pretty sure it was a sore point for him.

He finished eating and wrapped up the other half of the sandwich. "He wrote an investigative piece about the Army. Heads rolled. I was collateral damage."

A succinct but unrevealing response. "Don't you think it might be germane to this investigation?"

"In what way? It happened over two years ago. The main thing that strikes me is that I shouldn't have remained angry for this long."

"What about Ben? I got the feeling from what you said that he was annoyed with you, too."

"*Annoyed* would be an understatement. I was furious that Larry hadn't let me know that article was coming. Maybe I could have found a way to distance myself, but he sideswiped me. He was really angry with me that I couldn't understand his position."

He sighed. "Ben was right, though. If anyone had found out what he was doing, there'd have been a lot of pressure on the paper and maybe on Larry to squash it. Not that I'd have told anyone in so many words. Hell, I didn't even have to know what it was about. Just mentioning in an ear or two that something was coming and

that I didn't have any other clue might have been enough
to stall this storm. At least the part that dumped on me."

"So it ruined your career?" She folded her sandwich
wrapper and reminded herself not to make this sound
like an interrogation. He probably wouldn't like it, and
she didn't want to stem the flow of confidences now
that they were coming. She couldn't help the feeling
that they were teetering on the edge of something important. "How could it do that?"

"Easy. Don't rock the boat."

"But you didn't do the rocking."

"Doesn't matter. I wasn't involved in any way with
what Larry did. Hell, I didn't even know until the article appeared that any of it had happened. It sure as
hell didn't involve me or my troops, and it didn't happen anywhere in my chain of command. A few lower-
ranking men in another regiment were arrested, but
somebody way up must've been chapped. Or felt threatened. Anyway, I was an easy target. Nobody could have
touched Larry after that article was published. Maybe
they thought they could get back at him through me."
He shrugged. "Whatever. It's done."

She hesitated, creasing the waxy paper in front of
her until the edges were sharp. "How have they ruined
your career? You arrived here in uniform."

"I'm still in uniform and will be until I hit twenty
years. Then I'll be out."

She lifted her head, feeling seriously disturbed.
"How can you know that?"

"Because my performance reports sank. I should be
a lieutenant colonel in order to continue after twenty.
I'm now considered 'low retention,' which means I'm
definitely not going to be asked to stay on."

"But how can they do that?" Her feelings about this were starting to get tangled. She needed to understand.

"It's simple. There are a limited number of people who can get promoted. They don't find a slot for me, I'm on the way out."

"What did Ben mean by a star?"

His faint smile looked sour. "I was being fast-tracked and looking good to become a general eventually. I became a major early. Prospects were bright. Now they're very dim."

She let that sink in. As she thought it over, however, she could understand why he felt his career had been ruined. She didn't necessarily understand how all that worked, but he did. He was part of the machinery.

"I'm sorry," she said, feeling genuinely saddened.

"Me, too. And as the performance reports didn't improve, I got madder. Ben was right about one thing. I was being selfish."

The admission surprised her. "Why? Your career was wrecked. That had to be infuriating."

"Sure, but was that worth cutting off my brother? He'd done the right thing, but I didn't. I wish it weren't too late."

No way to answer that. No point in arguing against feelings. She sighed, then rose and gathered up the remains of their meal. "So now you want justice."

"I would have wanted it regardless. For Larry."

She believed him, felt a touch of his grief. "What a mess."

"Oh yeah."

She wiped up stray crumbs, then tried to smile at him. "Coffee?"

"I've intruded too much."

She put a hand on her hip. "I might have thought so earlier, but I'm not feeling that way now. This is important. I give a damn about Larry, and now I give a damn about you. You might not want it, but I care. So quiet down. Coffee? Or something else?"

"A beer if you have another."

As it happened, she did. "I buy this so rarely that you're in luck."

"Then why did you buy it?"

"Larry," she answered simply.

For the first time, they shared a look of real understanding. The sense of connection warmed her. She hadn't expected to feel this way, not when it came to Duke. Maybe it helped to realize he wasn't just a monolith of anger and unswaying determination.

As Cat returned to her seat, she said, "You put me off initially."

Another half smile from him. "I never would have guessed."

A laugh escaped her, brief but genuine. "I'm usually better at concealing my reactions to people. But there you were, looking like a battering ram. You sure looked hard and angry. Nothing about you made me want to get into a tussle."

He looked at the beer bottle he held. "Most people don't want to tangle with me. I can understand your reaction. I came through that door loaded for bear. Too much time to think on the way here, maybe."

"You looked like walking death," she told him frankly. "An icy-cold fury. Worse, in my opinion, than a heated rage. Scary."

"Comes with the territory," he said after a moment, then took a swig of his beer.

She could probably wonder until the cows came home exactly what he meant by that. Maybe it was better not to know. But she still had other questions.

"Duke? That article Larry wrote? Can you be sure it's not relevant?"

"It's been a while. Just over two years."

"That doesn't mean it can't fit into this."

He shook his head. "It was about a murder-for-hire scheme within the military."

Cat was taken aback. "Murder for hire? Someone wanted to get rid of someone else?"

"Not exactly." He put the bottle on the table and leaned back a bit. "There were apparently a few soldiers who were paid to eliminate certain Afghans. Contract killings. I don't know if it was ever discovered who paid them, but I do know they were all charged with murder. Larry uncovered the whole thing, and witnesses were willing to testify. At least the ones not in uniform any longer."

"My God," she murmured. "That's awful."

"Absolutely. A stain on the uniform."

"But why should that reflect on you? Did you know anything about it?"

"Not a thing until Larry's story broke." He leaned forward, and once again she caught a glimpse of the man who had walked into the office: hard as granite, angry. "If I had heard about it, I'd have done exactly what Larry did. Not in a newspaper, of course, but I wouldn't have let it go until I cut the rot from the tree. Ugly. Disgraceful. Cold-blooded murder."

Cat wasn't sure what Duke might have done to get himself out of the line of fire, but she could certainly understand why he had felt betrayed. To have the story hit the press and not even be prepared for it?

But at the same time, she had no difficulty understanding why Larry had chosen not to say anything.

"Do you suppose Larry might have thought he was protecting you by not including you in any way? Given what happened to you, maybe if you'd been able to send out a warning that the story was coming, people might have wanted to know why you didn't stop it."

His gaze grew distant again, as if he was reviewing the past. "It's possible," he said. "I didn't think of that at the time, but it's possible. On the other hand, when we had our argument, he never once said he was trying to protect me."

Well, cross that out, Cat thought. She needed to move, to mull this over.

"I need to change out of this uniform," she announced. "If you want, head down to the basement for a workout. I'm sure it's not what you're used to, but if you don't have to run in the rain, why do it?"

She heard a wind gust as she walked from the kitchen, rattling windows and flinging raindrops around. Not a great day to be outside unless you had to. Right now she didn't have to.

After a hot shower, she changed into some warmer clothes, including a blue flannel shirt. The weather had made the day colder, and her house as well. Drafts crept everywhere, and she thought about closing curtains to settle them down. Nah. Whatever was left of the day's light, she didn't want to shut it out.

In the kitchen, she discovered that Duke had washed the coffee mugs. Courteous guy.

As the borrowed heat from her shower wore off,

she still felt a bit chilled. She went to the living room, turned on a few lamps, then curled up beneath a knit blanket on one end of the couch. Her book still rested on the end table, and she picked it up.

This case, she thought, was sprouting potential complications. Tomorrow she'd go to the office and catch up on what they'd learned. Right now, however, it was time to relax.

She heard a clang from below that told her Duke was working with her free weights.

Peace for a little while.

Out in the rain, wearing camouflaged ponchos, three men sat in their gully and watched the creek rise even higher. It was too wet for a fire, which meant they couldn't even make coffee. Alcohol lamps could heat their rations a bit, but not make any decent coffee. Unless they wanted cups of instant.

They were used to the discomfort, but that didn't mean they liked it. At least with the cover of rain, they could walk a little, stretch out the kinks from being cramped so long.

On the other hand, the dropping temperature and the dampness reminded them of abuse their bodies had suffered over the years, of old wounds and battered joints.

"Ah, hell," said Man One. "We've got to figure out what we're going to do next. This rain won't last forever, and it'll wear out as an excuse pretty quickly."

"Who's gonna know?" asked Man Three. "Seriously. This takes as long as it takes, and if they don't get that, we need to refuse to go any further. It's not like this is an enforceable order."

The second guy spoke. "I like the money. Do you?"

"Hell, yeah," said the third man. "But we're operating under some pretty tight constraints here. And some pretty bad intel. We don't know exactly what we're looking for."

"Any information he might have wanted to use in that book he was writing."

The first man, who'd been listening, spoke. "But we don't even know what it was about. Someone has a suspicion, obviously, but without telling us, we can't know for sure if we've found it."

The second man jumped in. "I suspect," he said sarcastically, "that we'll know because it mentions the Army somewhere."

"Or some officers," suggested Man Three.

They all nodded, agreeing on that.

The second man spoke again. "Here we are, sitting in the damned rain again, freezing our cojones off—"

Man One interjected. "Don't exaggerate. We've been in worse."

Man Two answered him. "Yeah, man. We have. But my point still stands. We're not *doing* anything. We're not even sure how to proceed. Staging a series of break-ins that look like some teenage fools did them is fine as far as it goes. But we wanted to do the jobs after dark when no one was home. We didn't want anyone to be able to say they saw big masked men. Hell, we don't want anyone to suspect these actions are anything except robbery."

"So here we sit," said Man Three. "I don't like it, either."

Man Two threw a pebble into the blackened firepit. "We already killed one man. Larry effing Duke. Do you really think they sent the body away because they didn't suspect torture? We can't leave a string of murders behind us."

The first man picked up a thin stick and flexed it, as if to test its springiness. Beneath his poncho hood, he didn't look any happier than the other two. But happiness wasn't a prerequisite. They had a job, and now it was time to figure out how to complete it. After a bit, he threw in his two cents.

"We'll leave murders behind us, but only if there's no other way. This was supposed to be a clean, quick op. It's not. Who would have guessed that Larry Duke would have refused to give us the info? I sure didn't. But we'd have had to kill him anyway."

"I'm not arguing against that. I'm just pointing out that the whole idea of waiting for these buddies of Larry's to leave town overnight isn't going to pay any dividends. How many of them do you see taking trips? How long are we going to wait?"

"I don't know," Man One said. "But I'm going to place a call soon and find out if our mission has changed, or if there are any better suggestions because of what we learned. We didn't come out here suspecting we'd need to pay a visit to anyone but Larry."

"Intel failure," said the second man. "A serious intel failure."

"We *know* that," said the third man.

The first man threw the stick he was holding. It fell into the rushing creek and vanished. "The thing is, nobody thought Larry would be able to withstand questioning like that. How many have you known who could?"

"His brother is a Ranger," said Man Two. "Maybe it's in the genes."

"That's ridiculous," snorted the third man.

The second man just shook his head. "Who would have expected such resistance from a reporter, for Pete's sake?"

Man One spoke. "It's irrelevant what was expected. We have to deal with what is. Now put your brains to it, men. It'll probably be sometime tomorrow before I can get someplace we can get a cell phone signal."

Which was kind of surprising to them all, considering they had a satellite phone. This was a communications dead zone for some reason. Or maybe the satellite phone was screwed up.

"Did anyone consider he might have left his research back in Baltimore?" asked the third man.

Man One answered, "I suspect I'll get that ball rolling when I call tomorrow. Just think, men. Try brainstorming ideas. If we're stuck with burglary, then we'll have to figure out how to do it without alerting the entire damn region to our presence."

With that they all fell silent, but irritation and gloom filled the air around them.

Not even a tent to cover them. Oh, it sucked.

Chapter Four

Duke refused Cat's offer to take him back to the motel. The rain had let up a bit, and despite his workout in her basement, he still felt a need to run.

He wasn't exactly dressed for a workout, but he didn't care if he got wet or sweaty. He didn't care about much except his brother.

Maybe his focus was getting too narrow. He wondered what he could learn from people who had played poker with Larry. Probably not much. If the cops had questioned Larry's poker mates, if one of them suspected anything of the others, they probably wouldn't remain mum.

He was pretty damp by the time he passed the sheriff's office and reached Mahoney's bar. Not so wet that he decided against going inside. Another beer was in order, and maybe some of the patrons would talk to him.

But the whole damn idea that he could just talk to people around here and learn something was beginning to look stupid to him.

Why in the world would anyone tell him something

they hadn't told the cops? Because he was Larry's brother? Right now that didn't seem like much of a reason.

Feeling truly grumpy, he walked into the bar. He'd been out of his mind when he came here, swamped in grief and fury and the need to do *something*. Anything for Larry other than put him in a casket.

Inside, Mahoney's felt like an old-time pub. Dimly lit and bigger than he'd expected from the outside. A couple of dartboards and two pool tables could be seen through a wide door at the back of the bar portion. Wooden booths and tables filled the front end. Nice. It was filling up for the evening, mostly with men, and all of them talking to each other.

He took an empty stool at the bar and lifted his feet to the rail. A chubby man of about sixty came down the length of the bar and scanned him with sharp dark eyes before smiling and saying, "I'm Mahoney. What can I do you for?"

Duke took a chance. He extended his hand across the bar. "Daniel Duke."

Mahoney responded with a firm grip while saying, "Any relation to Larry Duke?"

"I'm his brother."

Mahoney's face sagged. "I'm sorry, Mr. Duke. Really sorry. I didn't know Larry for long, but he was a great guy. Made friends fast and made a lot of people laugh."

"That's how I remember him."

Mahoney nodded, seemed about to say something else, but finally chose the safest thing. Hard to talk to someone who was grieving, Duke thought. "What can I get you, Mr. Duke?"

"Everyone calls me Duke. And whatever you've got on tap."

"Be right back."

There was a big mirror over the bar, even in the dim light catching the glimmer from liquor bottles. The mirror was probably as old as the establishment, showing signs of losing its silvering in scattered spots. Mahoney returned a minute later with a big glass filled with beer and foam. Duke liked the foam, always had.

"On the house," Mahoney said. "I suppose you want to be left alone."

Duke shook his head. "I was hanging around thinking I'd like to meet some of the people Larry knew. A few stories might do me some good, and it would be nice to know that Larry had friends in the area. Cat Jansen told me he used to play darts here."

Mahoney smiled. "He was a mean dart player. He must have played it for years. It got so folks who watched him started placing dollar bets on whether Larry would lose." Mahoney chuckled. "Think about that. Not whether he'd win, but whether he'd lose."

Duke felt himself grinning. "Definitely Larry. I never could beat him in a game." Which wasn't strictly true, but it didn't matter. "And people still played against him?"

A twinkle came to Mahoney's eye. "You bet. After a beer or two, a challenge can become irresistible."

Duke laughed outright. He knew the mentality.

"Everybody liked Larry," Mahoney said. "That's why this came as such a shock." Then he looked around and called out, "Merritt? Can you come over here? I want you to meet someone."

Duke twisted his head and saw a big guy who looked like someone who worked outdoors a lot get up from a table he'd been sharing with two other men. He wended his way over with a loose gait.

Mahoney introduced them. "Merritt, this is Daniel Duke, Larry's brother. Duke, Merritt was one of them fools who was always trying to beat Larry at darts."

Merritt laughed and stuck out his hand. "I used to be the best darts player in this bar. Not after Larry came." He slid onto the stool to Duke's right. "I'm sorry about your brother, man. He seemed like a straight-up guy and funny, too. And the puns? He raised them to a new art form. Had to be careful or prepared when you were talking to him." Merritt's eyes creased with a smile.

"Larry was good people, although his knack for puns sometimes nearly drove me up the wall."

Merritt nodded. "I get it. You'd be sailing along in a conversation, and he'd make a pun on some word or other. Then everyone would crack up, and the conversation would get derailed. But it was always fun." Then he shook his head. "I don't get why anyone would want to kill him."

"Me, either." Which wasn't entirely true, because Larry had gotten knee-deep into investigations that might have made someone angry enough. But none of them were here.

He swallowed some beer, thinking. No, of course none of them were here. Larry had come here to write a book, and while that might be a useful cover, it wouldn't be about this place. Hell, he couldn't imagine anything around here that would draw the attention of a reporter of Larry's stature. Sure, there had to be crime and corruption, like everywhere else in the world, but nothing big enough to reach Larry's radar.

Merritt spoke again. "So were you big brother or little brother?"

Duke summoned a smile. "Little brother. Larry was two years my senior. Didn't keep us from being tight, though."

Merritt paused long enough to raise a finger to Mahoney. "Let me buy you another beer. Then you come join me and my friends. If you want, we can reminisce about your brother. It was a short time, but it was a good time. Would've liked it to be longer."

"Me, too." Truer words were never spoken. Mahoney brought a fresh draft for Duke and a new bottle for Merritt. Then the two of them wound their way to the table near the back where the two other men were looking curious.

"Larry Duke's brother," Merritt said to them, his thumb pointing backward to Duke. "Just call him Duke, he says."

The two, introduced to him as Dave and Rich, were friendly enough, although maybe a bit cautious. Duke could understand. Maybe they feared an outpouring of grief.

But his grief was private, and he preferred to keep it that way. He'd nurse it in the quiet, dark hours and keep up whatever other appearance he deemed necessary.

Dave and Rich told him what a great guy Larry had

been. Duke found himself remembering how he'd suggested to Cat that people might be franker with him because he knew Larry was imperfect. So much for that pipe dream.

Never had not speaking ill of the dead seemed like a heavy weight. How to get past it?

The other two men joined Merritt in talking about Larry's skill at darts. "He was pretty damn good at pool, too," Dave said.

"That's interesting," Duke said. "He never mentioned that he played."

"He sure did," Rich said. "Really good at it, so he must have done it a lot."

"Larry said it required being able to see vectors and forces, whatever he meant," Dave announced. "Never saw a guy make a ball curve around another the way he did, and right into the pocket. He should have played competitively."

But Larry wouldn't have enjoyed that. He had undoubtedly learned and used it as a tool. Duke nodded but remembered his brother's passion for investigating and writing. A very real passion. Just like Duke's passion for the Rangers. Duke wasn't as interested in getting a star as he was in being able to keep the job, which challenged him to his limit, mentally and physically.

Merritt spoke. "Larry was a reporter, right?"

"Yes," Duke answered. "One of the best. He did a lot of investigative pieces, some of which were pretty dangerous work."

The three other men exchanged looks. Then Dave said, "Wooee. He never mentioned that."

"He didn't like to brag." Duke sipped more beer, slowing down his consumption. Getting drunk wasn't on his menu for the night. "He was fearless, though."

Duke, who had a dangerous job himself, decided he might not have paid enough attention to Larry's courage. Not exactly something you thought of when it came to reporters.

But Larry had told him once the story of a female reporter in another state. The story had made Larry grin as he related it, but it wasn't truly funny.

The woman had uncovered some serious corruption in her sheriff's department. She'd been digging around for more information when the sheriff himself called her and said, "People disappear in the piney woods out here."

No, not funny, and the woman's editor had agreed. Larry's reaction should have revealed something to Duke, he now thought. Larry was used to threats. He'd said enough a few times for Duke to pick up on that. But to react that way to the woman reporter's story? Larry must have faced considerably worse.

And Larry treated it as if it was all part of the job. *Hats off to you, Larry.*

His three companions fell silent for a bit, drinking their beers, and Duke wondered if he should move on. He didn't want to become oppressive, or to make anyone uneasy. Strangers could do that if they hung around too long.

At last he rose and thanked them all. No one stopped him, but he caught the furtive glances of sympathy. They were feeling bad for him and didn't know how to act. The situation had to be uncomfortable. The dead man's brother, a guy they didn't even know, sitting here with them.

Well, that would put paid to a night of fun.

"Say, Duke?" Merritt stopped him. "Come on back when you can. I'm here most evenings since the wife left me for a bull rider."

Duke looked at him. "Seriously?"

"Seriously." Merritt shook his head. "Anyway, no need to be a stranger."

"I won't." On the way out, he thanked Mahoney for the beer and received another invitation to return.

If they were hoping he'd be the life of the party the way Larry could, they'd be sadly disappointed.

Outside the rain had become heavier again, joining the deepening darkness to partially obscure the far side of the street. How apropos.

Cat was standing at her front window staring out into the renewed rainstorm as night blew in with it. A battered pickup pulled up in front. Then the driver climbed out and dashed toward her door. Under his rain hood, his face was concealed.

She heard the inevitable knock, and she went to answer it, positively in no mood to be disturbed. When she opened her door, she changed her mind. It was Ben Williams, and he wouldn't have driven all the way from his house through this rain for casual conversation.

"Hey, Ben," she said, trying to paste on a smile. Her mind was still half in the novel she'd been reading until a few minutes ago.

"Sorry to bother you, Cat, but I've been thinking about Duke's visit. The department told me you were here."

She gestured him inside with a movement of her head and led him to the kitchen table so she could offer him something. It only seemed neighborly. "Should I make coffee? Or I might have a beer left." She actually thought she had two, but she was beginning to wonder if she shouldn't drink another herself.

"I don't want to put you out."

Duke had said the same thing. She must be walking around with impatience written all over her. "You're not," she lied. "Have a seat. Beer or coffee?"

"Neither, thanks. If you want some, go ahead. I'm fine."

Given the hollow look in his eyes, Cat figured Ben was anything but fine. She ached for him, for his sorrow.

She sat across from him, wondering if she needed a bigger table. She'd never figured it would get this much use, but then, she'd never imagined working at home. Nope, that was what she had the department's office for.

"What's up, Ben?"

"I'm not sure. I used to know Duke."

"I kinda gathered that when he said he introduced Larry to you."

"Yeah." He nodded then sighed, a shaky sound. "We didn't tell him about us, though. It must have come as a shock to him."

"He wondered if you were the same Ben Williams. He was pretty sure you were. But I didn't get the feeling he had a problem with it."

"Maybe not. Larry and I had to be secretive when I

was still in uniform. Things were bad enough for me, and Larry worried about it. We kind of crept around."

Cat frowned, her pain for this man growing. "That's horrible, Ben. Just horrible that you guys had to do that. I'll never understand it. Your personal relationship didn't affect anyone else."

"In theory. My parents sure didn't like it when I came out. Not a word for ten years now."

Cat shook her head and sighed heavily. "I don't know what to say except that's awful. I'm so sorry, Ben."

"I'm mostly used to it. I disappointed them, they kicked me to the curb, and after all this time..." He shrugged. "Their decision."

"Maybe they'll come around."

"I don't think I'd ever trust them again. Anyway, part of the reason I'm here is that I hope to get to know Duke even better because of Larry. If he still wants to talk to me. Plus, there's nobody I can talk to around here. Larry did a good job of keeping us private." He met her gaze almost as if he was making a plea. "I know I shouldn't lean on you this way, but..."

"You need someone who knows about you two. So you can talk freely."

He nodded. "Not fair to you, I know."

"Fairness is something we make. Besides, I really liked Larry, and he told me about you. Not much, but I knew. I guess he trusted me."

"I would say so." He sighed. "I honestly don't know what Larry was working on, but I think Duke wants to know. Did you guys find any hints at his house?"

"Afraid not, at least not yet. We're still evaluating

evidence. But his computer was gone. I can't tell about much else."

Ben's head snapped up. "His computer? Who kills to steal a damn computer?"

"Good question." The more she thought about it, she felt that might be a pivotal question in all this. A bunch of kids who wanted to steal electronics would wait for the house to be empty. Wouldn't they? It was certainly a poor excuse for a bloody murder. She closed her eyes. It *had* been bloody. She really didn't want Duke or Ben to see the scene.

Then she looked at Ben again. "Why would he care what people around here thought of your relationship?"

"I don't know. I didn't expect it when he told me he was taking a sabbatical out here to write a book. Silly me, I was expecting picnics, hikes, dinners together…all that romantic stuff. Well, I got something quite different."

Cat's chest tightened. "That stinks."

"Yeah. But Larry was Larry, and I was used to his secrecy. I figured he had a good reason. Sometimes I even wondered what he thought he was protecting me from. If he was."

"That's also a good question." Ben had given her two points to put in the mental mill for processing. Hopefully some kernels would pop out of all the chaff.

"Anyway," Ben continued, "I was surprised by being kept out of sight. It left me wondering what he might be working on, though he wouldn't say, no matter how many times I asked. I quit asking. Anyhow, the year I was anticipating with the love of my life turned into two months, and they were…difficult. For me, at least."

Cat had no trouble imagining how that must have felt. "It would kind of make me wonder what kind of relationship we had."

"The thought crossed my mind."

Boy, did Cat feel bad for him. Relationships inevitably had their ups and downs, but to be kept out of the good things? To be relegated to a back room in Larry's life?

For the first time, she didn't think so well of Larry. "Did he spend *any* time with you?"

"He'd come over at night a lot. We'd share some beers or wine, cook together, spend hours just lolling around gabbing. It wasn't every night, though. Two months may not be enough time to judge long-term, but he *really* wanted me not to be connected to him."

Cat didn't have to say that was terrible. Ben already knew.

Still, the secrecy was another layer on this case. As outgoing as Ben was, she'd have expected him to squire his boyfriend around town. Instead Larry had shown up at least a couple of times a week to have a drink or play darts. Not fair at all to Ben to be left out. That must mean something. She made another mental note. She might have to question Duke about it. Great. Most of the time that man did a great imitation of the Sphinx.

"I have some idea how it feels, Ben. I lost my mother about the time *you* moved here, but I'm sure it wasn't as bad as what you're going through." Useless words, but she needed to address this man's grief.

"I heard. You nursed her, right? Really tough."

"But I knew what was coming. I had time to say all

those important things, and to show her. You didn't even get that."

He nodded slowly, then wiped under his eyes as if tears had overwhelmed him. "Damn," he said presently. "I keep crying."

"Anybody would. Let it flow." She rose and brought back a box of tissues to place in front of him.

He gave her a muffled thanks and wiped his eyes a few more times. "I didn't mean to dump on you. I just needed to talk to someone, especially about Duke. What does he want?"

"Justice for Larry. I think I'm supposed to keep him from wrecking the case. He was sure loaded for bear when he got here."

Ben wiped his nose, then reached for another tissue. "That would be Duke. He's a battering ram." Then Ben shrugged. "That's part of the job."

"Were you a Ranger, too?"

"I didn't try, honestly. Wasn't for me. I met Duke over in Afghanistan, though. I was on a patrol and we met one of his units, and there he was, striding along with his men. That night we all shared a camp, and Duke and I became friends. We met up a few times when we got back to the States. One of those times he introduced me to Larry, who was in town to visit him."

"I'd wondered, the way you two talked."

"We weren't best friends, but we could sure have a good time knocking back some beers."

Cat tried to imagine Duke having a good time and failed. Of course, that wasn't a fair judgment under the circumstances. "And Larry?" she asked.

"We hit it off like a house on fire. A couple of weeks later, we were together. Secretly, of course."

Too many secrets, Cat thought. Entirely too many. First to protect Ben while he was still in the military, then hiding an investigation from Duke that had caused him serious problems, and now more secrets. To protect Ben again? No way to know now.

Given Larry's penchant for playing it close to his vest, she had to wonder what other kinds of secrets he might be hiding. A chill trickled through her. Not because she suspected Larry might be a baddie, but because now she had to wonder who else he might have crossed in his career. Especially recently.

Again, no way to know. Frustration began to build in her.

Ben spoke. "I don't know what Duke thinks he can do that the sheriff's department can't."

"I think he wanted to talk to people who'd met Larry. He thought people might be franker with him than with us."

"Not likely," Ben said sourly. "Larry didn't tell anybody anything. At least not about his work. At this point, I wouldn't be shocked if he had an ex-wife somewhere."

Ouch! Cat's sympathy rose another notch.

"Not that I think he did," Ben hastened to say. "But the last few days, I've been wondering what else he might not have told me. Pointless."

"I know. I'm sitting here wondering the same thing."

Ben sighed. "I'm sorry I'm taking up your evening. I'll go home now, but I want to talk to Duke some more. We may still have to iron out a few things."

"I'll tell him." Cat walked Ben to the door and watched him drive away over pavement that glistened beneath streetlights.

The weather had nothing on the storm she felt brewing.

THE RAIN WAS really beginning to annoy the three men in their gully. They'd had to move up the slope because the creek was so engorged, and now they sat with their boot heels dug in to keep them from sliding down into the rushing water.

"This wasn't a good idea," the second man said. "I know the gully conceals us, and we'd be able to move down it to cover if we needed to, but that damn mountain forest doesn't look quite as thick now. We could have maneuvered among the trees."

"Not as well," answered Man Three. "Come on. We've been through worse."

"I didn't retire to do this all over again."

The first man didn't say anything. If he sighed, it was lost in the pouring rain and the rushing of the creek. Bellyaching was part of a soldier's coping mechanism. He mostly ignored it.

The second man spoke again. "We can't do a damn thing tonight to finish this mission. That's bothering me more than the effing weather. I want this done and over with."

"Face it," said Man One, speaking for the first time in over an hour. "We've got a serious case of mission creep going on here. If you two would stop complaining and start thinking, we might get out of here sooner."

"Yeah?" asked Man Three. "What is your huge brain telling you?"

"That we need to be even more cautious. We need to be able to break in without the homeowners or kids waking up so we don't have to be on indefinite hold. Has anyone thought of halothane?"

"Like we can get any out here," snorted the second man. "And how are we supposed to aerosolize it to fill an entire house?"

"I wondered about that, too. Anyway, thinking ahead, I brought a big canister, a tube and a mister that should do it. It's in my truck."

The other two fell silent, maybe stunned by the first man's prescience. Halothane, a surgical anesthetic, could put people to sleep for a little while. In theory it wouldn't kill them unless they got way too much.

"Why didn't you say so before?" asked the second man.

"Because I didn't want to use it. It'll leave traces in the blood. It's not easy to come by, so that would point in two directions—a hospital and the military. How many directions do we want these cops to be looking? Two isn't enough. And it sure doesn't point to a bunch of teenagers."

"Hell," muttered the third man.

"So try to think of something better," suggested the first. "I just threw it out there to stir your brains. Find a way around the halothane. Don't just sit here and moan."

"But you've really got it?" asked the third man.

"Absolutely. But it's the last resort, hear me?"

They heard. They understood. They didn't have to be happy about it, though.

Chapter Five

The morning brought sunshine and crisp air. The storm of the day before had caused the springtime temperatures to drop enough that Cat wondered if they might get more snow.

It wouldn't be unusual at this time of year. She loved the changeability, especially in the spring and autumn.

She considered wearing her uniform, then decided against it. Running after Duke mostly wouldn't call for it. And if she needed it later, she could put it on. One way or another, it wasn't going to be a day at the office.

She phoned him as she stood on her small front porch and waved to people driving to work. He answered immediately.

"Duke." Crisp, no nonsense.

"Hey, Duke. You ready to start the day?"

"Sure. I'll need a shower first. Just got back in from a run."

She couldn't resist asking, "So was it a run or a jog?"

She thought he snorted, but she couldn't be sure over the phone.

"It was a run. Where should we meet?"

"I'm hankering for a latte, so Maude's it is."

"That's the City Diner?"

"Yeah, but everyone around here calls it Maude's."

"I can see why," he replied dryly. "Give me twenty, please."

Presto, change-o, she thought as she tucked her phone away. Better take her car in case he got a wild hair. It would have been a great morning to enjoy a run of her own, except she had one problem Duke didn't: she was known to almost everyone. Privacy didn't exist for Cat on the street.

The morning breakfast crowd had begun to trail away by the time she arrived. There was one group of older men who had turned Maude's into their meeting place and always sat in the back. Generally they were too busy talking among themselves to pay much attention to anyone else.

Cat exchanged waves with them and took a table right in front of the window. A few minutes later, Maude appeared with a tall paper cup. "Latte, right?"

"You know me too well." At least Maude didn't slam it down the way she would have slammed a coffee cup. "Thanks."

"That new guy coming along? The one you're babysitting?"

Cat nearly froze in surprise. How had that gotten around? Loose lips in the department? "Where did you hear that?"

"Don't recall. You know how things float around here."

Amazing Maude said so much. A warning of some kind? She had the feeling that Maude, per usual, wouldn't say another word about it, so there was no point in asking. Maude had already turned away to stomp back behind the counter and wait for a customer who needed her to tromp back into the kitchen.

Given that Duke had already been out on a long run, she suspected that would be soon.

Sipping her latte, she waited and watched the street. More pedestrians were appearing, particularly women who seemed to be hurrying on errands. There was a small party store down the street, patronized by people who had a child's birthday coming up, and a very small organic food store that somehow was hanging on when there never seemed to be anyone walking in or out. At the far end of the street sat a meat-processing place where you could bring your deer in the fall or a steer you wanted to use to feed your family. They'd even age the meat to make it taste better.

On weekends, a small vacant lot turned into a farmers' market. As much good produce as could be raised around here. The environment for it had never struck her as the best, but people still managed.

Then she saw Duke striding down the street toward the diner. Of course—a long run followed by a walk. It was a wonder the man could ever hold still.

As soon as he came through the door, before they could do much more than exchange greetings, Maude appeared at the table to slap down a menu. "Coffee? Black?"

"Black, thanks."

After Maude brought it, she groused, "A big man like you needs to eat. Figure out what you want."

Duke stared after her, the corners of his mouth twitching. "She'd have made a good drill instructor."

"I wouldn't be surprised. *Have* you eaten?"

"Not yet." He sipped coffee then picked up the menu. "What about you?"

"Toast and peanut butter. My favorite since childhood."

"Sounds good. But I saw your basement gym. You could use a bit more than that toast. I think I see turnovers up there with the pies." Then he astonished her with a wink. "Maybe some doughnuts, too."

She laughed. It was an old joke, but most cops tried to enjoy it anyway.

He ordered a full-on breakfast plus a turnover. She suspected it was for her.

He spoke to her as he set aside the menu. "Are you incognito today?"

"Not really. Trying to draw less attention to you, but my badge is on my waist. Ben showed up at my house last night. He wants a chance to talk to you again."

Duke nodded. "Fine by me. Maybe we can share some good memories. But he didn't recall anything else?"

"Only how secretive Larry was, even after he arrived here. It seems he kept Ben under wraps, which was not what Ben expected at all."

Duke frowned. "I wouldn't have expected that of my brother."

"After what Ben told me, neither would I. I mean, I didn't think much about it when Larry told me Ben was his boyfriend, but I never really thought about not seeing the two of them together."

"I knew they flew under the radar before Ben resigned his commission, but that was the last I heard about it. Six months after Ben left, Larry and I had our...rupture. I guess the two of us really need to talk. Big blanks."

Shortly, Maude brought a heaping plate of scrambled eggs, breakfast sausage and home fries, with a side of ham and the turnover. "You want more, it's on the house."

"Thank you," Duke said. After Maude had walked away, he asked, "Where did that come from?"

"Her steadily softening heart, I guess. She probably heard you're Larry's brother."

"So much for a low profile." He pushed the apple turnover toward her. "Yours."

"Thank you." What else could she say? He'd done something nice for her, and she hadn't refused when he'd suggested it. Besides, as her mouth watered, she decided it was unlikely to add five pounds.

She pulled a napkin out of the dispenser and drew the small plate closer. Apple and cinnamon. The aroma was wonderful. The first mouthful was delicious.

"Anything else?" Duke asked after a bit, when his plate was half-empty and the ham was gone.

"Apart from the odd secrecy? One thing. When I told Ben that Larry's computer was gone, he remarked that seemed strange, to kill someone over a computer."

Duke's head lifted. "That was it? His computer?"

"There may be other things. I don't know yet. I was

pulled off the case because I knew Larry. Obviously. But it got me thinking. That was an awful lot of violence for one laptop."

"Damn it, Larry," Duke growled quietly. "What the hell did you get yourself involved with this time?"

Cat couldn't answer. Nobody knew the motive for this murder, nobody evidently knew what Larry was working on and, given his natural secrecy, it was unlikely anyone in this area knew he was gay.

Duke went back to eating, but this time clearly without pleasure. He was eating for fuel, nothing more.

Cat eventually spoke, the turnover mostly gone. "We can't be sure it had anything to do with his work. Maybe he just ran into a bad actor. It can happen, Duke."

"Yeah." But he didn't sound as if he believed it.

Neither did she. There was an awful lot of violence. Someone had to be seriously angry with Larry to do that. But she didn't want Duke to get wound up again, not when he was being so cooperative with her. If he went out of here carrying a lance with blood in his eye, she didn't want to think about what might happen.

Gage had given her permission. She could share what she thought necessary. Given that, she needed to direct Duke.

"I'll call around, Duke. I'll see how many of the people who played poker with Larry are available to talk to you, and when."

"Okay. Thanks." He nodded and went back to eating like a kid whose mother had told him to clean his plate. He might have lost his appetite, but he wouldn't waste food. She liked that. She absolutely hated wasting food.

She was probably the only person around here who could have a meltdown when she discovered a rotting green pepper at the back of her fridge.

Okay, not a meltdown, but she always felt bad.

Maude swung by to refill his coffee and ask if she wanted another latte. Duke answered for her. "Sure she will. She may deny it, but she does. She can take it with her."

"Duke!" Cat felt a bit of annoyance. "I can make my own decisions."

"I know you can. I also know that you try to be polite. That's been obvious. If you can't drink it all, that's okay, too."

Man, he had her number, she thought when he insisted on paying the bill. She at least didn't feel uncomfortable about that. He'd ordered the turnover and coffee without listening to any objection and without getting her permission.

Served him right. It wasn't like Gage had suggested she use an expense account. Why should she? Duke was an uninvited complication.

She decided not to go back to the office, but to take Duke to her house once more. She would have peace to make phone calls, and she wasn't sure that any of the poker gang would be free before evening. If any of them even wanted to talk to him.

Back at her house, she paced as she made calls. First was to Gage.

"I'm going to take Duke around to talk to the poker group, unless you object."

"That seems harmless enough. We already got everything they could share or were willing to. Just pay attention in case he teases out something interesting."

"Will do." Cat hadn't expected a different answer, but this was one way to keep Gage up to date on Duke's activities. He *had* asked her to keep him informed.

"One other thing," she continued. "Nobody knows what Larry was working on. And Ben Williams commented how strange it was that someone would take only Larry's laptop. Did we find anything else missing?"

"His phone. These days everyone has a smartphone. We couldn't find one."

That sent a trickle of unease running down her spine. "Damn," she murmured.

"Yeah," Gage answered. "You didn't know that?"

"I got thrown out of there because I knew him, remember? I shouldn't even be on the case."

Gage snorted. "I use what I got. Anyway, we haven't released the scene yet. I sure as hell hope we can find if something else is gone. It might be a clue."

"How are we supposed to know?"

After she disconnected, she wondered if she should even tell Duke about the phone. Wait, she decided. Just wait. And there was that big question: How were they supposed to know if anything else was missing? Other items, such as cash, no one would know about. From what she'd read in the reports, they hadn't found Larry's wallet, either. But all those things could fit with a robbery.

Except Larry's horrific murder.

She felt Duke watching her from the kitchen. She

turned to look his way. "The scene hasn't been released."

He stood. "You said it had been."

"I said it *might* have been. Gage said we're still not through."

Duke frowned. "It's taking a long time."

"We're a small department. Nobody wants to overlook something."

He nodded but clearly was disturbed. "And the poker group?"

"I'll start making calls."

It took most of the rest of the day to reach everyone on the list. She felt as if Duke would be happy to start with just one, but that would delay setting up the rest for meetings. She just kept plugging away until she had two appointments laid out.

"Was everyone agreeable?" Duke asked.

"Some of them even sounded eager. None sounded reluctant. Only two could schedule at this time."

"Good starting point. When's the first?"

"Matt Keller this evening. He owns the organic food store. He said he'd come over here tonight around seven. Next is Bud Wicke, tomorrow at lunchtime. We can meet him at the garage."

"And the rest?"

"They'll probably spread out over a few days. They'll call me."

Duke nodded.

"Mostly evenings. Most of them work, and only one is retired."

"Okay," Duke said.

"Why don't you get comfortable?" she asked. She was convinced he intended to remain planted here until Matt arrived. He must be worried that he might miss something.

He followed her into the living room, and at her suggestion, he sat at one end of the couch. She settled in the Boston rocker that her mother had loved so much.

After a few minutes, he spoke. "I'm wasting my time."

"How so?"

"You already questioned the poker group."

"You felt they might share more with you."

He shook his head impatiently. "They knew my brother for only a couple of months. What sounded like a good idea when I flew out here is beginning to sound less so."

Surprised, she studied him, wishing this man would be more open about his thoughts. "You want me to cancel the meetings?"

He shook his head again. "I've only got three weeks. I need to use them wisely, and I seem to be blowing them away. The problem is, I can't think of another line of attack. I *want* Larry's killer."

She ached for him. Her professional detachment insisted on draining away. She couldn't afford to let that happen. "We should go see Ben again. If you talk with him for a while, something new may emerge. Of all the people who knew Larry around here, he's the one with the most knowledge."

"Yeah. I want to see him again, anyway. But I can't keep spinning my wheels."

While she sympathized, she also knew something else. "Duke? This isn't my first murder investigation. I can tell you something you might not like to hear, but it's the truth."

"What's that?"

"Sometimes, however much evidence you think you've found, it's not enough to identify a killer. But then, seemingly out of nowhere, a new piece drops into the puzzle, and you're off and running. Patience is part of this job."

After a few beats, he nodded.

Cat also realized she wasn't going to be able to sit here like this and wait for Matt Keller to show up. She looked at her watch. Four thirty. There was time.

"Why don't we go to Mahoney's?" she said. "It's been a long time since my breakfast, and he makes great BLTs. Maybe have a beer, since I've been in that mood since Larry's murder."

He was agreeable. In deference to time, they drove in her car.

"I should drive my rental over here," he remarked. "At least my knees won't be ramming my chin."

She laughed. For the first time, it felt good.

THE GUY THEY were working for could only be contacted at night, so the first man had to wait. His call this morning had been dismissed with a brusque "I told you. After 4:00 a.m Zulu only." 9:00 p.m local time.

That hadn't made anyone happy, but they had to deal with it. The way they'd spent so much of their lives dealing with whatever happened, whether they liked it or not.

Then the second man let out a "Yesss!"

The other two looked at him. He was still obsessively holding Larry's cell phone. He waved it. "I found some names and numbers. They weren't on his contact list, but in his reminders list. They all have local area codes."

The third man nodded and smiled. "We'll get them now."

The first man wasn't as delighted. "We have to locate them. Then scope out where they live and figure out how to get in without being seen. And we still don't know what the hell to look for."

After a few minutes, the second guy spoke. "It has to be a flash drive."

"Why?" demanded the first man. "We were talking about reporters keeping notes on paper because they couldn't be hacked."

"I was thinking," the other man answered. Man Three chortled sarcastically, but the second man ignored him. "Thinking," he repeated. "If you're going to give someone a bunch of information to protect or hide, you're not going to give them the paper. You're going to copy a lot of the crucial stuff to a flash drive and encrypt it."

They regarded the idea almost glumly.

"A flash drive won't be easy to find," said the third man. "How will we know if we have the right one?"

"Take as many as we find. Bet they're near a computer, where they shouldn't stand out."

"Or between the mattresses, or in the cupboard,

or…" The first man trailed off. "Better than where we were yesterday."

"Marginally," Man Three remarked. "Hell. But at least we've got a starting point."

Man One rubbed his face with his hands. "Let's get that fire up again. I want me some coffee." Then he zeroed in on the second man again. "Find anything on that computer?"

"Hardly. Didn't I tell you the battery is dead? I need a plug. Recharge it or run it on AC."

The third man spoke. "Just don't tell me you don't have the adapter or the recharger."

"I got them. But I gotta plug it in."

Man One leaned back while Man Three tossed some dry twigs on the fire. Soon it was crackling but not smoking.

"Okay," said Man One. "That's the easiest of our problems. We can charge it at Larry Duke's house tonight, depending on whether they've still got a cop watching it. And speaking of Duke? His brother's in town, I heard earlier."

"Daniel Duke?"

The first man nodded.

"Damn," said the third man. "It's like playing whack-a-mole. Start to solve one problem, and another springs up."

After that, no one spoke at all.

Mahoney's proved to be just the pick-me-up that Cat needed. The country music wailing quietly in the background, the voices of people talking and Mahoney's warm greeting and his promise to give them the best BLTs.

Mahoney put a cold diet cola in front of her and a large glass of draft in front of Duke.

The place still hadn't heated up for the evening, so it was relatively quiet. Soon after five, the bar would be jammed.

Duke spoke. "This the only watering hole around here?"

"No. There are roadhouses around the county, serving scattered ranches. I imagine they did better in the days when every ranch employed a lot of cowboys. And there's one only a few miles outside town. Local bands play, it has a dance floor, that sort of thing."

"Popular?"

"Oh yeah. Can't beat the dancing, for one thing. A lot of the college students head out there for that, but they have a good mix of customers."

Mahoney brought the sandwiches, one for her and two for Duke, and conversation between them flagged. In the lull, Cat looked around and realized some of the patrons were staring at Duke.

Had they heard who he was and why he was here? Given the local grapevine, she thought that might be it, though she harbored a fleeting hope that maybe a few of them wanted to talk about Larry. If that was the case, she hoped she wasn't putting a damper on it.

While they ate, more patrons began to drift in. By the time they finished eating, the bar was at least half-full.

The hum of conversation had grown stronger, and occasionally laughter punctuated the background noises. A good night was on the way at Mahoney's.

Cat would have liked to kick back, enjoy a couple

of beers, then go home to her basement gym and take a stab at working off her sins, but no. She was driving, first of all, and secondly, the man beside her seemed to be getting a bit restless. Probably impatient for the conversation he was awaiting with Matt.

"You in a hurry?" she asked as he finished his sandwiches.

"Sort of. Not really. Hell, we got time."

She glanced at her watch. "Yeah, but that's not necessarily a reminder that will make you less impatient. We can go if you need to move."

He turned his head, looking across his shoulder at her as he leaned into the bar. "I used to enjoy spending an evening like this."

"With friends. That's different."

"Probably. Or maybe I'm just feeling like I'm wasting time."

He might be, she thought. Even he had lowered his expectations for these meetings. Justifiably so, considering she truly believed that these poker buddies would know nothing they hadn't already shared in interviews with the police.

She spoke. "Your brother's secrecy didn't help."

"I think he meant it to protect. And not just his sources. But yeah, he's a blank slate in that regard."

"Tell me more about the story he did. The one that affected your career. It might have some clues in it."

He shook his head, and she thought he was going to shut her down. Then he said, "Not here."

"Okay, then. Time to go home." She was surprised

how easily she used that word, including him in it. Not "my home" or "my place." Just *home*.

Dang, she thought as they walked out to her car. How had he gotten past her barricades? She'd hated this assignment, distrusted him, and now she was taking him *home* with her.

Egad.

THEY STOPPED AT the gas station and bought a six-pack at Duke's suggestion. When they got back to her place, she started coffee in case Matt didn't want a brew while he was there.

Then she sat facing Duke across the table again. He seemed to prefer the kitchen to the living room for some reason.

"That article?" she reminded him.

"I didn't forget." He rubbed his nose and sighed. "It'll give you some idea of the kind of reporter he is. Was." The past tense came with obvious difficulty to him.

Cat waited, giving him time to shift his thoughts around. Grief was doubtless weighing heavily on him since she'd brought up the matter that had caused him career problems. More important, it had caused a rupture between him and his brother. He probably didn't want to talk about it at all.

But she was hoping for something, anything, that might provide a clue to Larry's killing. She doubted Matt was going to be able to provide it while they talked this evening.

She'd known Larry herself, the whole time he'd lived here, and had learned very little about him. Maybe, just maybe, some of the poker players might have learned something over the cards and chips. The kind of free-ranging conversation that could happen with a few beers and having a good time.

But how would they know it was significant? The department had already questioned them, and nothing useful had come up.

Then another thought occurred to her. It wasn't that they might feel freer talking to Larry's brother. No, maybe Duke knew enough about Larry to elicit other kinds of information. Maybe he had some questions to ask that the cops hadn't thought about.

Maybe.

She was still waiting for Duke to speak when her front doorbell rang. Matt had arrived ten minutes early, jacket open despite the cold, still wearing the short-sleeved white shirt and jeans he wore at the organic food market he owned.

Cat introduced the two men and this time guided them into the living room. She asked Matt if he wanted coffee or beer, but he said he was fine as he settled on the edge of her recliner.

Duke took the couch and Cat sat on the Boston rocker again. During her mom's last month, Cat had added some cheerful pillows to it, to cushion her mom's shrinking bottom and back. Cat didn't want to remove them. There were few enough good memories left in this house.

"How's business?" she asked Matt, trying to ease past the initial moments of strangers meeting.

"Good enough." He flashed a smile. "Plenty of kitchen gardens around here, especially on the ranches. They provide a lot of our produce, and it sells as fast as they bring it in."

Cat arched her brow. "I have to admit I wouldn't have thought organic foods would be popular here."

"You need to keep up with the times. Now the grocery store is carrying them as well." His smile turned crooked. "I suspect they want to put me out of business."

"I hope not!"

"Me, too." Then he turned his attention to Duke. "I'm very sorry about your brother. He was a good guy, lots of fun. A shark at poker, though."

Duke managed a faint grin. "If he played it, he was good."

"Yeah, he had something of a reputation for darts, too. Anyway, it didn't matter that he was fantastic at Hold'em. We all just had a great time, and since it was only for chips, nobody went away annoyed."

"So no money?" Cat asked, although she had already guessed the answer.

"Not even penny stakes. No, it was just for fun."

"Did Ben Williams ever play?"

"Ben?" Matt looked pensive. "I know him, but I don't recall ever seeing him at the games."

Cat fell silent, hoping Duke would ask his all-important questions.

Duke spoke. "Larry ever tell you what he did?"

"Yeah," Matt answered. "Said he was a reporter, some paper back East. He said he was working on a book. But I don't remember him talking about it much. Just in passing."

"So you weren't curious?"

Matt shook his head. "Not my business. I don't pry, Duke. A person tells me what they want me to know. God, it feels funny calling you Duke. How'd you get the last name and not Larry?"

Another smile tried to be born on Duke's face. "My military career," he said. "Everyone started calling me Duke. It stuck. Before that I was Dan."

"Larry mentioned you once. He was awful proud of you."

That seemed to startle Duke a bit. But he said, "I was proud of Larry, too. Tough career."

"That's something, coming from an Army Ranger." Matt sighed, then leaned forward, resting his elbows on his knees. He looked down at his folded hands. "There must be a reason he was killed, but damned if I can figure it out. As far as I know, no one around here was mad at him. I guess that leaves kids who wanted something valuable and went too far."

"There was another break-in," Cat remarked. "Just the other day. No one was home."

Matt nodded slowly. "I heard about it. Burglaries have never been a common problem around here, but they happen every so often. Still, a group of kids wanting electronics or valuables... Why would they kill Larry?"

"I think we're all wondering that."

"Yeah."

For a half minute or so, they all remained quiet. Cat wanted to make sure Duke had a chance to ask any questions he needed to, so she let matters rest.

Duke spoke again. "My brother was an investigative reporter."

Matt sat upright. "Really? Hell, he must have had some stories to tell. He never said. Was he good?" He caught himself. "That didn't sound the way I meant it."

"It's okay," Duke answered. "I was just wondering if he'd said anything about his job, more than just that he was a reporter."

"Not around me." Matt put his hand to his chin, then dropped it. "You think it had something to do with that?"

"I don't know," Duke replied. "I wish I did."

"But doing investigative stuff…he must have run afoul of people."

"It's possible."

Matt thought about it, then shook his head. "He didn't say anything to me about his work. Not even what he was writing a book about. Maybe it had something to do with his reporting?"

Duke gave a small shrug. "I wish I knew, but Larry never struck me as the type to try to write a novel."

Now, that was a bit of information they hadn't had before, Cat thought. It seemed Duke still thought the book might be an investigation. As far as she knew, no one else had thought that to be relevant. Writing a book sounded like an innocuous thing to do.

But considering how angry Duke had been about a story that hadn't even been about him, she could imagine a whole lot of reasons that others might have been even more furious. Or might think they had something to fear.

The fear idea nearly made her jump up, but she held on to her cool, not wanting to halt the growing conversational flow between the two men. After all, it had so far yielded one potentially useful nugget, maybe two, and nuggets were rare in this case thus far.

Matt spoke first. "I gotta admit, the idea of Larry being killed during a burglary bothers me. It has from the time I first heard. It's kind of random, you know? I'll be the first to admit I never really got close to Larry. I mean, it was only a couple of months, and we didn't get to the confessional stage, just the level of being friendly and having a good time. I never got the sense that anyone hated him. And I never got the sense that he was trying to get information from someone, like he was working on a story. If he was, it wasn't one from around here."

Cat caught herself. "Okay, that almost made me laugh."

Duke jerked around to look at her. "Why?"

"Imagine an investigative reporter from a big daily newspaper actually spending his time investigating anything around here. I mean, man. Our paltry scandals would probably bore him to tears."

One corner of Duke's mouth lifted, and Matt smiled widely.

"Yeah," Matt said. "And since there are hardly any secrets in this town, nobody'd want to read the story anyway. A city council member was inebriated and had to be assisted to his front door? Joe XYZ, a teacher, is having an affair? Great gossip."

"And not worth wasting ink on." Cat nodded.

"Definitely not the stuff of headlines," Matt agreed. Then he sighed, and his face drooped. "Larry became a headline." He shook his head. "I'm still having trouble grasping it. And for you, Duke, it has to be a whole lot harder."

Duke spoke slowly, as if dealing with his feelings was tough. "Larry and I hadn't lived in each other's pockets for a very long time. We'd get together once or twice a year. He wasn't part of my daily life, is what I'm saying, but he was always *there*. Now I can't even pick up a phone to call him."

Cat understood completely. She still ached from wanting to be able to talk with her mother about most everything.

Matt left shortly, having offered nothing more about Larry's murder, but Duke seemed satisfied with the conversation.

Then Duke left a few minutes later, explaining that he needed to go for a run. He didn't look dressed for it, but Cat didn't argue. Maybe Matt had stirred up some of his memories and he needed to run off sorrow.

She had some other things to think about now, possibly useful things.

And she also needed more details on the second break-in. Was it related in any way to Larry's?

She was tired of being left in the dark.

Chapter Six

Duke hit the pavement, his booted feet pounding. No stealth there, but no reason to care about it. He'd get to the motel, change into his running gear and do his miles.

Maybe hit the truck stop diner for a late-night breakfast. He didn't figure Mahoney's BLTs were going to hold him all night. His calorie consumption had sometimes caused Larry's eyes to widen.

Well, hell, when you kept yourself in prime condition, worked out like a lunatic and had a lot of muscle mass to support, you ate a lot. More than average, anyway.

He'd also learned a long time ago that he lost weight while on a mission, so it didn't pay to start off too lean. Everyone lost weight in a war zone. Maybe it was the lousy food. Maybe it was the tension. Maybe it was as simple as troops not wanting to eat. He didn't know. He just saw the results.

Carrying a couple of extra pounds never hurt. But just a couple. If he ever stopped working out like a demon, he'd have to watch it.

Random thoughts, a meaningless diversion produced by his own brain. He was aware of it, the times his mind wanted to take a vacation from something. It could be dangerous under some circumstances, so he was usually good about stopping it.

But what did it really matter, right then? His grief over Larry was growing, not easing, and he felt like he had a crushing weight on his chest, as if his heart didn't want to beat again.

He jumped into his running clothes quickly: navy blue fleece workout pants—not shorts, because it was chilly out there. A long-sleeved white sweatshirt. Running shoes, which were at least a decent brand that fit.

The point of this was to heat up, not cool down.

The last thing he grabbed was a flashlight with an orange translucent cone on it. Because this time he was running toward the mountains, hoping to get some uphill work, and he needed to be sure cars could see him.

While he didn't much care about his own life right then, he *did* care about a motorist who might hit him. Why give someone nightmares for the rest of his life?

At first he jogged slowly to warm up his muscles, but, at the outskirts of town, with the mountains a dark silhouette against a sky dusted with stars, he hit his full pace, an all-out run.

He might have recalled nights spent in hostile mountains where he had to be alert for every little thing, nights when he'd slept sitting up with his rifle across his lap, nights when he'd been all alone and surrounded by threats or with comrades as uneasy as he was. Nights when terrible things had happened, things that he would never be able to expunge from memory.

He'd slipped down that path before, and sometimes he just let it happen, knowing he couldn't always stop it.

But not tonight. Tonight, Larry ran alongside him, residing in his memory, his easy laughter still audible in Duke's mind.

He'd never hear that laugh again. He'd never again listen to his brother's laboring breaths as he tried to keep up with Duke's pace. They'd never again share a few beers and shoot the breeze for hours.

Never.

He hit an upslope, and his calves reacted as if they were glad to meet it. Power surged through him, sweeping him upward. The flashlight he carried gave him just enough light to see the ground ahead of him, to avoid obstacles.

Cars were few and far between, however. He'd expected more traffic, but maybe he wasn't on the state highway. He had no idea and didn't care.

He heard Larry as clearly as if his brother were running beside him. "Think about it, Dan."

Think about what exactly? That Larry hadn't been working on a novel? As far as Duke was concerned, that was a given.

That maybe someone had been afraid of what Larry was writing, or afraid of something Larry knew?

Likely. Larry had never made a big deal out of it, but Duke was aware that his brother had received death threats. How many or over what, Duke didn't know. Larry had mentioned them a few times but had always laughed them off.

"They just show me that I'm doing it right," Larry had said.

Well, yeah. Duke's career had been shredded by Larry doing the right thing. He was sure Larry hadn't intended that, but his brother was like a bloodhound on a scent trail. He wouldn't be diverted.

"Maybe you shouldn't have laughed them off, Larry," Duke muttered, keeping his breathing as even as he could. Deep, deep breaths, but regular. No oxygen deprivation allowed.

Duke was thinking as he ran uphill. Okay. That thing that Matt had said about maybe someone had been afraid of Larry... That could put a different spin on all this.

He'd seen Cat stiffen when that came out and was sure she'd had the same thought. Why would anyone here even consider the possibility? No one here, evidently, had the least idea of the kind of stories Larry had worked on.

Like all the time he'd spent on domestic terrorism, revealing links between some of the groups. Larry had mentioned he was still receiving threats a few years after the article was published.

What about other things? Duke tried to remember all the articles his brother had written, but the simple fact was he hadn't heard about any number of them because he'd been overseas for long periods. Impossible to really keep up, and Larry almost never mentioned his work on postcards or in the occasional telemeeting they had.

Not that Larry would reveal anything until his story was published, and even then he kept a lot close to his vest.

Duke was sure there were more kernels of information in Larry's brain than he could ever use in his published articles. Tips, clues, people, things he couldn't substantiate well enough to write about. But they'd all remain in the stew pot, because Larry never knew when one of his gleanings might prove useful at a later date.

Damn, Duke wished he had even a remote idea what Larry had been writing about. Maybe something had come together in a way that needed more than six or eight pages of newsprint. Something big enough to make it worth a few hundred pages.

It wouldn't surprise Duke to learn that.

He shouldn't be surprised if Larry's investigations had gotten him killed. The warnings had been there. But the idea was useless unless he could discover what his brother had been doing.

Crap.

Duke turned at the top of a long slope and began to run back down. Not as fast, because downhill was always tougher to negotiate without falling. But fast enough.

Larry. Damn it, Larry.

Duke had known his own job was dangerous, but he truthfully hadn't believed Larry's could be *this* dangerous. If it was.

That was the next thing he needed to figure out. He'd go talk to this other guy at lunch tomorrow, but he expected to hear pretty much what he'd heard from Matt.

Stupid idea, questioning his poker buddies. Except for one thing: that someone might be afraid of Larry.

After his own experience, Duke figured that wasn't

a far reach. Larry had exposed a terrible crime, murder
for hire, but Larry had walked away alive, and for all
that Duke's career had gone into free fall, he was still
here. Still wearing the uniform.

Apparently no one had wanted to stir that hornet's
nest up any more.

Unless maybe they had?

He was still wondering when he reached the truck
stop diner.

Cat sat on her small front porch. A molded plastic chair
cradled her, and she put her feet up on the porch railing.
A jacket protected her, holding the cool night air at bay.

She was thinking about the conversation with Matt.
About Duke, who couldn't wait to leave once Matt was
gone. He'd even refused her offer to drive him to the
motel.

The man was upset. Understandably so. Cat wondered if he'd yet felt the full impact of grief, or if he'd
been so furious and determined to find Larry's killer
that there'd been no room left in him for sorrow.

It might be that there was now.

Despite all her attempts to keep Duke at arm's length,
partly because of her job and partly because she didn't
trust that expression she'd initially seen in his eyes, she
had begun to care.

"Oh, cool," she whispered. Yeah. Just what she needed:
to become personally involved.

She was personally involved enough with Larry that
Gage Dalton hadn't wanted her on the case. A murder

investigation, something she'd done for her previous sheriff, and she was frozen out.

Maybe not totally. It was time to corner Gage and demand information. She needed to be kept in the loop, not only for herself, but so she could better assist Duke in ways that wouldn't cause trouble with the legal case they were building.

How was she to know what to keep him from plowing into if she didn't know the status?

If Gage had thought that herding Duke would be easier when she was wearing blinders, he was wrong. What was the chance that she would allow information to escape her? Zilch. She knew how to protect investigations.

She thought of Duke again, allowing herself a few moments to think about how attractive he was. She was a woman, she had normal impulses, and even in the midst of all this, she wasn't impervious.

Then she brushed such thoughts aside. Given the circumstances, Duke couldn't possibly entertain such thoughts, nor should *she*.

Then there was Larry. Whenever she thought of Larry, she pictured him smiling. A big grin, filled with the joy of life. A man who should never have been the target of a killer.

Maybe she needed to talk to Gage about the fact that she couldn't read any of Larry's articles. She'd tried once, searching his name online, but the articles were in the paper's archives, behind a paywall. It hadn't seemed worth the money when she'd just been curious.

But it might not be curiosity now. If Gage authorized it, she could call the paper and say she was investigating

Larry's death. Right now she didn't have the authority to say any such thing, but it might be important to learn what the man had been doing.

All she knew about Larry was that he was a friendly, outgoing guy, and that she'd liked him a bunch. He'd been a wide-ranging conversationalist, able to talk about many things comfortably and always eager to learn something he didn't know. Never afraid of admitting to gaps in his knowledge.

When she thought about it, she realized he had gotten her to talk more with him than she usually did with anyone. He'd brought her out of her introverted shell easily.

A great gift for a man who spent his professional life digging information out of people, many of them reluctant to speak.

Determined to speak with Gage in the morning, she let her thoughts drift more freely.

That Duke was like a puzzle box. She'd been seriously worried about what he might do when he'd arrived here, and now she was getting more worried about *him*.

So far he hadn't given her any major headaches, but if he felt he was getting nowhere, if he was left to deal with his grief without a resolution, how would he handle it?

Would Duke feel as if he'd failed his brother in this final, monumental task? Would guilt overwhelm him because this whole ugly mess was worsened by his rift with Larry?

She didn't understand how anyone could handle it well. A double heaping. She'd seen other people hit with this double whammy, though. Mothers who'd fought with a kid before the kid disappeared, only to be found dead. That was just one example. She'd seen plenty of others.

People dealt because they had to, but Duke was a man of action. He'd already shown that he wasn't prepared to wait for the police to do this job.

She sighed and rested her head in her hand. All she wanted to do was help. That had been her motivation in becoming a cop. She hated it when she couldn't.

OUT IN THE COUNTRYSIDE, three men sat in a different gully. Moving was always wise in case someone had sighted them and started to wonder. New digs, no better than the old ones, but at least far enough away.

The chill didn't bother them much, and besides, they had the correct clothing. Dark jackets covered them; hoods covered their heads and shadowed their faces from the rising moon. After a brief debate, they'd decided to build a small fire and now were making coffee in a battered tin coffeepot.

They used water warmed on the fire to soften dried foods enough to eat and swallow. Not the best grub, obviously, but marginally better than rations. Evidently companies catered to hikers and campers who insisted their food be palatable. Sort of.

Anyway, there was no grousing that night. Just a lot of silence as they tried to think their way through their current conundrum.

"We could kill Dan Duke," said Man Three.

"Oh, for crap's sake!" growled the second man. "We're supposed to stay under the radar, and you want to kill the brother of the man we just murdered? You don't think that would send up a dozen flares?"

Man One, who hadn't said much for a while, spoke quietly. The other men sometimes resented the fact that the first man seemed to think he was smarter than they, never mind that he patently was. It was when his tone and pacing grew obviously patient that they resented him most. Right then he was sounding patient.

"We need to get a charge on that laptop. The cops are still watching Larry Duke's house."

"They've been there too long," groused Man Three.

"Maybe," said Man One, growing even more obviously patient, "they're concerned about ghouls. Especially teenage ghouls. Word must be getting around that the guy was tortured. Or at least that the scene is gruesome."

"I wish we were plugged into the local gossip," said Man Three.

"Wishes and horses and all that," said Man Two.

Man One didn't disagree. "The real problem here is lack of intelligence. We didn't expect all these complications, and we sure as hell weren't prepared for them. But this isn't some backward country where we can operate freely."

"No kidding," said the second man. "A lot of places we've been, I'd just take out the guard, go into the house to charge this freaking laptop and do whatever else I want to. Not here. Kill a cop, and we're up to our necks. Kill Dan Duke, and we're in it big-time."

The third man spoke. "I know Duke is supposed to be some kind of big deal, but what kind of big deal?"

The first man answered tautly. "I'd give you his service jacket if I had it. Just know he was being fast-tracked for the top, and not only because he knew the right people. That was the least of it. When the military history books are written, his name will be in them."

The third man spoke again. "I take it you don't mean because he eventually gets a star?"

"No. His commendations would fill a book. He's reputed to be a tactical genius. He's faced everything that we have, and probably more. Some think he should get the Medal of Honor for one mission."

The second man blew air through pursed lips. "I hadn't heard about that." Then he turned toward the third man. "The point is, we've *all* heard about him. Even you. That should tell you everything you need to know."

The first man spoke again. "We're not talking about just going up against somebody's brother. If we have to, we will. But I wouldn't advise it. The man could be capable of taking out all three of us."

Another long silence fell. The coffee started perking, and the second man leaned forward to move it to the side of the fire. Twigs and branches crackled as flames danced through them.

"And we can't do another break-in?" asked the third man.

The first man sighed. "We can. But first I want that damn laptop charged. We could conceivably save ourselves a whole lot of trouble."

"Except for what Larry Duke said about us never finding the info."

"He could have been lying."

They all hoped so.

It was so much clearer on an operation overseas. Here it was all muddied by lines they couldn't cross.

Nobody had considered these parameters.

CAT EVENTUALLY ROSE, deciding to go indoors. The evening had been peaceful, few people about, but the chill was beginning to penetrate by way of her hands and denim-covered legs.

A cup of instant cocoa sounded perfect.

Inside, she boiled some water in her kettle and pulled cream out of the fridge. She always liked a bit of cream in the instant cocoa. It tasted richer.

When the kettle began to whistle, she poured the hot water into a mug over the mix. An easy, relaxed evening would continue.

A twinge of guilt hit her as she remembered the exercise she was forgoing, an hour or so in her basement with weights and her bicycle. It was okay to skip a couple of nights, and it wasn't as if she needed to work out any tension.

Then her thoughts returned to Duke. Sitting at her kitchen table, she wondered about him running along the roads of this county, dealing with his demons, missing his brother. Should he even be out there alone?

Remembering his palpable anger when he had arrived in town, she wondered if he should be alone with that, either.

Damn, that man wouldn't stay out of her head. She told herself he had to be her priority right now, but she

suspected that was an excuse. Despite his initial anger, he'd steadily drawn her in. She cared about the hell he was dealing with, about how he was handling it.

Well, when she got additional information tomorrow at the office, she might have more she could safely share with Duke. One thing she *didn't* want him to know was that their initial assessment was that Larry had been tortured. God, she didn't want to be the person who had to tell Duke that.

Forgetting her relaxing evening, she put her forehead in her hand and stared down into her cup of cocoa. What happened to Larry had been awful, just awful, even without all the details. She couldn't imagine how much more awful it would be for Duke to know.

Finally she sipped her cocoa again, then thought about tossing it, because it had grown cool already.

The rap at her door startled her. The digital clock on her microwave said it was just before ten. An emergency? Heck, this town practically rolled up the streets by nine, if not earlier.

Concerned, she hurried to answer the door. When she opened it, she was astonished to see Duke. The breeze had picked up, and even though he stood a few feet away, she could smell soap and shampoo.

"Come in," she said, quickly stepping back.

"It's late…"

"You're here for a reason. Come in."

He passed her, heading straight for the kitchen. She followed him, then asked, "What is it about you and kitchen tables?"

He shrugged. "In our family, this is where we always

held conversations. Larry and I kept it up even sitting at tables when we went to a bar."

That made sense. She faced him at the table, pushing her mug aside. "What can I do for you?"

"I just had a question. When I saw your lights were on, I thought it might not be too late to knock."

"It wasn't. Another half hour might have been different."

He half smiled, reminding her of how attractive he was when he wasn't on the edge of fury. Something had changed since he'd talked to Matt.

"I'm beginning to realize I'm probably on a futile quest," he said after a minute or two.

Surprisingly, her heart squeezed. Not what she wanted to hear, despite all her initial objections. The fact was, she was now looking at a man who wasn't accustomed to being stymied. How much harder for him than the average person. Nor did she have any reply to reassure him.

He continued. "I was reacting to Larry's death. I needed to do something. My usual reaction to crisis. Useless under these circumstances."

"I understand it," she admitted.

"Still, there's reality, and I've been avoiding thinking about it. There are so many situations I've encountered where I've been able to do something. But to act, you need to know the parameters of the situation. You need intel. I don't know why I thought I could wring more out of people he knew here than you and the other cops could."

He shook his head. "But I was sitting there, talking

with Matt, and it struck me that the folks Larry played poker with know the cops around here better than they know me. The idea that they'd say something to me that they wouldn't say to you all…well, I must have been out of my mind."

"Grief and shock will do that."

"Yeah. I should know that. I'm sure you do, too."

Cat shrugged one shoulder a little bit, then waited. She was convinced he hadn't come here to dump some uncomfortable feelings. She judged him to be a man who was largely buttoned up.

He seemed lost in thought, his gaze distant, and she wondered what had been so urgent that he'd come to see her this late. Maybe being alone was difficult for him right now? She began to think about offering him the single bed in her home office.

He suddenly zeroed in on her. "The reason I came over."

"Yes?" She couldn't help tensing.

"Is there any way I can get more information, about what you know? About that second robbery that Matt mentioned?"

She nodded. "I was planning to talk to the sheriff in the morning and ask. Whatever I can share, I'll tell you."

"Thanks." He looked down at his hands.

There was more; she could feel it. Then it struck her she hadn't offered him the most basic of courtesies. Dang, her mother would be disappointed in her. "Want something to drink? Obviously I've got beer, because you bought it earlier. Or instant hot chocolate. Or coffee, if you're one of those people who can drink it right before bed."

He made a snort that sounded like an almost laugh. "I learned to drink coffee round the clock. Strange how it doesn't seem to interfere with my sleep even when I'd like it to."

She had to smile. "So what'll it be?"

"A beer, please. Or I can get it. I've been here often enough to know the way to your refrigerator. Strange, I can see it right from here."

She laughed. "Okay, help yourself."

"What about you?"

"No, thanks. I prefer my head to be clear. My usual limit is one drink."

He rose and got his beer, returning to his seat as he twisted it open. No bottle opener for this guy.

"So that's what you wanted to know? If I can find out something else about Larry's case?"

"Not quite." He tipped the bottle back and drank before he spoke again. "What Matt said about fear. I sensed you noticed."

"Yeah, I did." No point in denying it.

"That would put a whole new spin on this. What's the point of looking for the killer around here if he might have been in and out? Sent by someone who had a grudge against Larry because of his reporting or was afraid of what he might write."

"I agree. So tomorrow I'm going to see if I can use my badge to get past his paper's paywall and read Larry's articles."

"Hell, I can get you past the paywall. Let me get out my credit card."

"You can't wait?"

He shook his head. "That's not what I meant. I just meant you don't have to use your badge or the department's resources. That's all. I was going to try to get into his archives anyway. I'd like to have copies of all those articles and exposés."

"I'm sure. Now I would, too. But I need to do it in official capacity. What if there's some kind of evidence in there? That article you two fought over? Do you think it could be that?"

"I don't know. I need more to go on. But it's possible. It's also possible he was working on something else and that story was over two years ago. On the other hand…"

She waited, then prompted, "Yes?"

"On the other hand, who knows how long that trail was? I told you about the guys who were charged as a result of that story, but who knows what information they might be willing to trade?"

She sorted through that. "But if some guy agreed to offer information in exchange for a lighter sentence, there'd be nothing for anyone to protect now."

"Maybe not. Or maybe someone is afraid of what else Larry might have known. But again, it could be any of his stories, or even a new one."

She thought about it. "But if he keeps everything secret, no one would know what he might be working on now."

"Not exactly. The people who gave him information might know. And maybe one of them got nervous and told someone else. Maybe we focused too much on his secrecy."

She became totally alert as he offered another new perspective. Maybe... But how to use this?

"We still have a lot of questions," she said. "And if we do find out something, how are we going to locate his sources? I'm sure Larry must have protected them." Even facing the difficulty of the task, her excitement continued to mount.

Duke answered. "Oh yeah. Protected better than classified information is my impression. I don't know if his editors even knew who most of his sources were. Never discussed that with him."

Cat changed her mind and got up to get herself a beer. "Want another?"

"Haven't finished this one. Thanks."

Cat brought her own beer to the table, glad she wasn't sleepy any longer. She'd needed this boost, a rush of adrenaline, the idea that they might have a direction to head.

She was driven hard by the desire to find answers, the need to catch the perp... Those were her fuel.

She stared down at the icy bottle in her hand. It wouldn't stay cold for long. "You can't pour beer over ice," she remarked.

The craziness of her words brought Duke's thoughts to a sharp stop and startled him into a laugh. "What?" he asked.

"Irrelevant," Cat answered. "Just one of those nutty thoughts that occur to me sometimes. I don't know why. Maybe it's a mental vacation."

She had a really sweet face. That was his own irrelevant thought, given the circumstances. But it *was* a sweet face, those blue eyes of hers bright, almost seeming to glow. He'd watched microexpressions pass over that face tonight, but they were slight and brief, and he had no read on what she was thinking right then.

"You can't pour beer over ice," he repeated. "That sounds strangely profound. Maybe you're trying to get at something."

She shook her head a little. "If I am, I suppose it will rise to the surface eventually. If it does, I might never make the connection." The barest of smiles appeared on her face. "Or maybe I'm just honestly thinking that this beer is icy right now, but it's not going to stay that way."

"Maybe."

He studied her, wondering at his own responses to her. Or maybe they were just normal *because* of the circumstances. Seeking a diversion, seeking an affirmation of life, wasn't exactly outside his experience.

Whatever. The fact that he found her sexy wasn't fair to her. He had a strong sense that she preferred to be judged on her other merits.

He turned his attention back to Larry, unable to dispel the feeling he'd been unwilling to acknowledge thus far: she knew something she wasn't sharing with him.

He understood that she couldn't tell him a lot of things. But the way she had reacted when he'd said he wanted to see Larry's house? That had been niggling at him, despite the reasons she'd stated. How could they still be treating the house as a crime scene after all this time?

Since he hadn't known Larry's address here, he couldn't even find the house. Conard County was a big, largely empty patch of earth. Look at how far out of the way Ben's house was. Without an address of some kind, he doubted he'd have been able to find it even with GPS.

So why wouldn't she let him see the place? When he'd argued that he'd seen a lot of horrific things during his career, her response had been to point out that those things hadn't involved his brother.

But they *had* involved people who had been his friends, people with whom he'd had the close bonds that could only come about from relying on one another in life-threatening situations.

Trust. Deep brotherhood, a kind different from what he had shared with Larry.

He sipped more beer, telling himself he'd achieved what he wanted, that he didn't need to take up more of her time. She'd promised to seek information and share what she could. However much she could share would be more than he had now.

As long as he wasn't beating down doors or threatening anyone, or going where the cops hadn't yet gone, he couldn't see a serious problem.

But it was still time to leave. He'd already busted up whatever had been left of her evening. Not much of an evening, but still hers.

He started to push his chair back.

"No," she said.

"No?"

"No," she repeated. "You can have my spare bedroom. It's a little on the small side, and my office stuff is in there, but you're welcome to it."

The invitation surprised him. "Why?" he asked bluntly.

"Because." She shrugged and offered a fugitive smile. "Because," she said again. "You're a stranger in a strange land, and while I'm sure you're used to it, you still don't need to be alone with your grief. So stay. You're not an intruder anymore."

Not an intruder? An interesting way of phrasing it. Deciding to accept her kindness, he slid back to the table.

"Thanks," he said. "You must want to go to bed."

"Not any longer. I'm wide-awake now."

His fault, that. "I should have waited until morning."

"Nah. I was thinking about the similar things, too. Nice to hash it out a bit. Good to know you reacted the same way to Matt that I did. I'd been considering tons of motives, most of them pretty standard for murder, but I hadn't considered fear as a motivator. Seems like an oversight now."

It did, Duke thought. It certainly did, given Larry's reporting, but... "I didn't think of it, either. It should have been the first idea that occurred to me."

Cat frowned. "I usually think of fear when a wife kills her husband. I'm not always right, of course, but when there's been abuse, then I think of it. Maybe it's time to put that in my complete rucksack of reasons."

"You might never need it again unless, like you said, there's domestic abuse."

She rose from the table and started pacing the small

space. "It should have occurred to me sooner, given…" She trailed off.

She was concealing something. His certainty grew. "Tell me how my brother was found again." He was sure she could tell him that much, because she had before. Maybe she would let more slip.

She stopped pacing. "Simple. Ben couldn't reach Larry, so he called us, and we did a wellness check. And there needs to be a better term for that sometimes."

Her face darkened in a way that unsettled him even more. What wasn't she telling him? "And?"

"Larry had been dead approximately two days. I'm sure the medical examiner will have a more precise TOD. Time of death. Sorry. When I'm in cop mode, the abbreviations come naturally."

"That's okay. I've got plenty of my own."

"So yeah, we went over there thinking he might have taken a fall and couldn't get to the phone. Broken leg, cracked skull or something. I wish."

Duke waited, hoping she might continue to talk, hoping she might let another detail slip. After a bit, he asked, "Did *you* respond to the call?"

"Yes," she said tautly.

He prompted even though he could feel her rising tension. "It was bad. Finding a body after two days can be disturbing."

"I've seen it before."

"So there *was* more."

"Damn it, Duke! Quit trying to get me to say something I don't know for a fact."

That told him too much. Enough. He could see her

jaw working, and now he gritted his own teeth. *Damn it, Larry. Damn it.*

His stomach plunged like he was on a roller coaster. He wanted to pick up his beer and smash the bottle against something. Smash his way back until the world righted itself somehow. Not that it had been right since he'd received word of Larry's death.

"Look," she said finally, leaning back against the counter and gripping it so tightly that her knuckles turned white. "You've probably seen a lot of things that never cross the desk in a sheriff's office in a smaller town, okay?"

Duke closed his eyes, feeling fury rising until his gorge rose with it. It pounded through his head, throbbed painfully in his chest, and he really, really needed to smash something.

He couldn't do that. Not now, not here. He drew several breaths, steadying himself. When he opened his eyes, he saw Cat still leaning against the counter, but now she looked stricken.

"I'm sorry," he said. "I shouldn't have reminded you."

She still didn't relax. He ought to get out of here now, before he made it worse for her. He remained glued to his seat anyway. The rage had subsided just enough for him to carry on. Maybe he needed to run another ten miles. The road called to him.

She spoke, her voice still tight. "I'm okay. But I just revealed too much, didn't I?"

"Only that his death was messy." But there was more to it than that. He was certain now. And he still needed to work out the fury. "Can I use your weights?"

"Of course." Her eyes looked dull.

The whole thing was ripping at her, he thought. All of it. Maybe in ways that didn't occur to him because she was a cop.

Then she straightened and poured the rest of her beer down the sink. "The office is down the hall, second door on the right. Look around, find what you need. I'm going to bed."

He'd been dismissed, and he was glad of it. Neither of them could take much more of this tonight.

Chapter Seven

In the morning, the sun burst from the east and painted the world in pink and gold light. High cirrus clouds turned into beautiful streamers of color against a sky turning deep blue.

It should have been a good morning to be alive, Cat thought as she drove to the sheriff's office. She had no idea what Duke planned to do that day. He hadn't emerged from bed yet, maybe because he'd pumped iron for a long time last night.

She didn't care. Except she did. This whole situation had begun to feel like her brain was on a hamster wheel, running around from one notion to the next.

Okay, so she didn't *want* to care. Fine. Too late.

Last night hadn't helped one thing that she could tell. She'd been cast back into the horrible hours after she and Guy Redwing had found Larry. She could tell that Duke had connected the dots, and that was her fault. She didn't feel good about it, either.

She had tossed and turned for a long time, hearing the occasional clank of iron plates from the basement. At least that had been a momentary diversion from her grim thoughts. She had eventually fallen asleep to the punctuation of that clanging.

She had no idea how much sleep she had gotten, but this morning her eyes felt sandy, and even though she drank two glasses of water, her throat felt parched.

When she parked at the sheriff's office, she considered heading to the diner for a morning latte. Yeah, why not? Better than being tempted to drink Velma's acidic brew.

Ten minutes later, coffee in hand, she walked into the office. She'd worn her uniform this morning, and she was struck by how much more secure she felt inside it. Maybe that was a hang-up all its own.

Inside, her fellow officers greeted her, and when she asked Velma about Gage, Velma pointed down the hall. The sheriff's office must be open for business this morning.

Gage was, as usual, behind stacks of paper and the computer he sometimes cussed because it couldn't read his mind. A common problem with machines.

Gage looked up immediately and waved her to a seat. "How's it going?"

"I'm asking you," Cat replied. "And I think I slipped up last night and let Major Duke know that his brother's death had been messy."

"The understatement of the year." Gage leaned back, his chair creaking.

"You need some oil," she remarked.

"I need a better chair. Thing is, I know all the problems with this one and how to adjust myself. A new chair would be a whole new learning experience."

She laughed. "I hadn't thought of that."

"Or maybe I'm just resistant to change."

"Not that I've noticed, at least not when it comes to something important."

He nodded, his dark eyes still trained on her. "What's up?"

"I want to know about the Larry Duke case, and about the burglary two days after."

One of Gage's eyebrows lifted. "Why?"

"Because I need to know more than what I saw when I arrived on scene. Because I need to give Duke some additional information. Because I need to know where we're at, what I can share and if I need to keep him away from something. Right now I'm wearing blinders."

He nodded, then winced as he leaned forward to put his elbows on the desk. He picked up a pencil and tapped it lightly, one of his favorite thinking poses.

"I get it," he said after a moment. "But why the second burglary?"

"There's always the possibility of a connection of some kind. The homeowners were out of town, right?"

"True."

"So maybe they're still alive because they weren't there."

Gage sighed. "Yeah. It's crossed my mind. Maybe most everyone's."

"See why I need to be clued in? No point in me running over things the rest of you have already considered."

He tapped the pencil more rapidly. "I'm going to have to trust you when it comes to sharing with Duke." He wasn't asking.

"Yes, but you know me well enough by now. I've been a cop for over ten years. I get the point of keeping investigations close to the vest."

"I know. I know." He dropped the pencil and once again leaned back. This time he didn't grimace. "I was trying to make it easier on you, but I guess I didn't. How are the two of you getting along?"

"Well, I no longer think he's going to kick in a door and start shooting."

He laughed. "That's an improvement. When I first met him, all I could do was wonder how we were going to restrain this tornado. Short of throwing him in a cell without charge."

"I honestly think he could break out."

"Maybe. Okay, get the files. Read them. I'm not even sure I know all the details myself."

"Thanks. One other thing. I need to read Larry's news stories, and there's a paywall. Can I approach in official capacity?"

"Sure, or use the department's credit card."

She rose, then paused. "Any idea when we'll get the autopsy and forensics?"

He shook his head. "They keep promising that it'll be soon, but soon hasn't come yet. I can't nail them down to anything more specific."

"Probably the most interesting autopsy they've done in a decade."

"Maybe. Or maybe they just don't want to chance missing something when this case is so gruesome and we're short on clues."

It was as good an explanation as any, she thought

as she headed out front to grab a computer. She could read the articles from home. The files? Not so much.

She paused just long enough to leave a message on Duke's cell. "I'm reading the files."

And probably unleashing a whole mountain of questions from him. This was going to be fun.

Not.

DUKE WAS OUT running again when he got Cat's message. The news quickened his pace without regard to endurance. He wanted to get back.

He'd stayed up late working with her weights. Then he'd added more repetitions. Trying to work through the maelstrom of emotions that wouldn't do a damn thing except cloud his mind.

Finally he had grown sleepy and had started looking for the bed and the bath. No clean clothes, so now he stopped at the motel on his way back from his run to shower and change.

Then he was off again. Remembering Cat had said something about a bakery, he detoured and found Melinda's Bakery facing the courthouse square.

"Hey," he said to the dark-haired young woman behind the counter. She had her head mostly covered by something like a shower cap.

"Hey," she answered with a smile. "Would you like lunch or pastries? At this point in the morning, the pastry levels have begun to shrink."

He looked in the case. "I bet you can hardly keep them full."

"For just as long as it takes me to fill the case and open the front door." She grinned. "I'm very popular."

He flashed her a smile. "Any idea what Cat Jansen likes?"

"Oh yeah. Turnovers and Danish."

"Then load me up with Danish, please."

She paused as she began to pull items out of the case and place them in a white bag. "I don't think I know you."

"I thought everybody within fifteen miles must know by now."

She laughed. "You've figured this county out. But no, I haven't heard about you."

He paused, then said, "I'm Larry Duke's brother."

Her hand froze as she started to fold the bag to close it. "Oh my gosh, I'm so sorry! He was such a nice man."

"He was." Duke hurried to pay, then left with his bag of delights. He wondered if he should take them to Cat at the office, then figured it would be uncivil of him to walk in those doors without enough to share.

He jogged back to her house and made coffee, then settled in for the wait.

CAT FINISHED UP by ten. It was disturbing to realize how little information they had about either case. Plenty of details, but little that was useful in finding a suspect. Were they going to have to wait until some item showed up in a pawnshop?

Hell, they didn't even know all that might be missing from Larry's house. Ben had supplied what he knew, but it was soon clear that he and Larry had mostly met at Ben's place. What was more, Ben was trying to cope with grief, they couldn't let him in the house and he had to guess about things that might have gone missing.

They definitely didn't want Ben inside that house. This was tough enough on him without adding nightmare images.

The Hodgeses' place was more informative, but hardly illuminating. However, that scene had been released. Maybe she should ask the homeowners if they'd mind if she brought Duke over. There was nothing there he could mess up in any way, and maybe he'd feel like he was doing something. Or that she wasn't trying to wrap him in a wall of silence.

Sighing, she finally gave up rereading for some nugget she had missed. She'd skipped breakfast this morning and just wanted to get home and eat.

She got one of the department's credit cards from the front desk, then headed out, hoping that Larry's articles might be more useful.

Maybe there'd be enough in one of them to kick-start an investigation at the other end of this trail.

Slim hope, because they'd have to offer some kind of link that wasn't as vague as "Larry wrote an article about…"

Crap.

She wasn't in the best of moods when she walked through her front door, but she saw Duke through the kitchen door, sitting at the table. Somehow that gave her a little lift.

She had a bigger lift when he held up the bakery bag, which always meant goodies.

He said, "Melinda packed it with your favorites. I made coffee. I know it's late for breakfast, but…" He shrugged.

"I haven't eaten yet. It's time for me." She felt a smile crease her face. "I hope you're hungry, too. This is fabulous."

Soon she had two dessert plates on the table, napkins and mugs of coffee. She was touched that he'd thought of such a thing, considering what he was dealing with.

"Did you go for a run?" she asked just before she bit into a raspberry Danish.

"Yeah. I needed it. I hope I didn't keep you awake last night. I tried not to bang around too much."

"You didn't." She'd had enough to keep her awake even if he'd never clanged a plate. "I'm sorry, but I didn't learn much this morning. Evidently there weren't a lot of clues in either house. Gage seemed to think both burglaries might be related. Anyway, the Hodges house, the second one, has been released, so I'm going to call them and ask if they'd be willing to meet you. They can tell you more about what was taken, and maybe their overall impressions."

"I'd like to look around." He settled on an apple turnover, eating with his fingers.

"I don't know if they'll give you carte blanche to wander around. Prepare to just talk."

"Yeah. But I want to ask if they knew Larry."

From the files she'd read, she wasn't sure anyone had asked that. In fact, the more she thought about it, it struck her as completely odd how little anyone had been able to discern from the crime scenes. Were they really down to forensics? No other clues?

Given how long it could take to get fingerprints through AFIS, it might take a week or more to get a complete check nationally.

Would anyone even want to do that at this point? They had no proof that someone from out of the area had committed the crime.

Duke spoke, his turnover gone. "You're thinking."

"Yeah. That could be dangerous."

His expression didn't leaven. "I doubt it. What's bothering you?"

"How very little evidence we have at this point. That may change with the completed forensics, but right now…"

When she left the thought incomplete, he spoke. "So both places were clean?"

"At the moment, that's how it seems. But more evidence will come to light. It always does." She wasn't exactly feeling hopeful, however. As she reached for another piece of her Danish, Duke caught her attention. He looked arrested, as if a thought had struck him.

"What are you thinking about?" Cat asked.

Slowly his eyes tracked back to her. "About how clean the scenes might be."

"And that tells you what?"

"Nothing yet."

God, now he was concealing things from *her*. If she didn't give such a huge damn about Larry and his murder, she'd run screaming from this whole situation.

Well, not really. She'd never been one to run scream-ing from anything. Still, the temptation was there.

"Damn it, Duke. If you've got an idea, share it."

"I can't. It's not exactly an idea. Not yet. I'll let you know once I've worked it through myself. About Larry's articles?"

"Yes. Gage told me to call the paper in my official capacity. If there's a problem with that, I've got one of the department's credit cards."

He nodded. "You'd think the paper would give me access, given I'm Larry's brother."

"Do they know Larry's gone?"

Duke grew grim. "Probably not. I guess I'll have to tell them."

"I'll handle that. And we'll get those articles today. I'm not going to be patient about it."

She just wished she knew what had caught his atten-tion about the scenes appearing clean at this point. That didn't necessarily mean anything. People had grown savvier about forensics thanks to television and mov-ies. Some of what they believed wasn't true, but, in her experience over a decade, more perps were leaving less of a trail behind.

She'd lost interest in her Danish but didn't want to offend Duke. He'd gone out of his way to bring her something she liked.

"As soon as I finish this, I'll call the paper," she said. "I'll have to wait until later to call the Hodgeses. Both of them are schoolteachers."

He nodded. "I'll survive." His smile was crooked. "Maybe I should try to extend my leave so I can drive you crazy a bit longer. Or maybe so I can relax a bit. I've set myself a tight deadline."

"It depends on the murder, Duke. Sometimes there just isn't enough information to point us in any direction. It will eventually turn up, however." She refused to remind him of how many stranger homicides that were never solved.

Then, hoping to get his mind going in another direction, she said, "*Can* you extend your leave?"

"I have enough time built up. My deputy can fill in for a while longer."

Amusement sparked in her. "You have deputies, too?"

That made his eyes dance. "Oh yeah. I could have said 'second in command,' I suppose."

"Then I would have missed my little joke."

"We wouldn't want that," he agreed.

She gave up on the Danish and rose to wash her hands. "I think I'll go dive into getting to Larry's articles."

"I'll be along in a minute."

Yeah, she fully expected him to be breathing down her neck and peering over her shoulder.

When she got to her office, she got a little start. She was looking at a twin bed made so neatly that she had to pause to admire it. He'd even squared the corners, something she never bothered with.

Duke had his advantages, she decided.

She knew the name of Larry's paper because he'd had a press card among his belongings. His wallet was gone, but a few things remained.

That could fit with a routine burglary: no cash, no credit cards remained. But the savagery of the murder made all that seem irrelevant. She closed her eyes a moment, unable to escape the memory of discovering Larry's body.

Stop! It wouldn't do a bit of good. *Work the problem.*

She reached for her landline, and when the paper's page popped up on the computer screen, she punched in the customer service number.

She hardly paid attention to the sounds from the kitchen, other than to recognize that Duke might be doing dishes. She had to work her way through three layers and finally landed at Larry's editor's desk. Lavinia Johnson. She scribbled the name down on her pad.

Evidently she was going to have to give the bad news first.

She identified herself, including her badge number, then dropped the bombshell bluntly. There was never a gentle way to deliver this news.

"I'm sorry I have to tell you, but Larry Duke was murdered."

"Oh my God!" The exclamation reached Cat across the telephone line, filled with shock. "What...? How...?"

"At this time it appears to be a home invasion, a burglary. But we're trying to check everything out."

"Of course, of course."

Cat waited for Lavinia Johnson to speak again, giving her a little time to absorb the news. She heard Duke come into the office and pull a chair over closer.

Then Lavinia spoke. "Does his family know? I have his emergency contacts."

"The news has been shared," Cat answered.

"I didn't want to have to make calls," Lavinia admitted. "Is there anything I can do?"

"We'd like access to the archive of Larry's articles."

"Do you think...? No, I guess I shouldn't ask that. Ongoing investigation. Yes, certainly. If you have a pen ready, I'll give you the newsroom's log-in and password."

"I'm ready," Cat answered. She scribbled quickly and repeated the information to Lavinia.

"That's it," the editor agreed. "Damn, I still feel like the world's spinning. Larry was a fine reporter and a fine human being. We're very proud of him here."

"I've heard wonderful things about him."

"Every one of them is true," Lavinia answered. Her voice was growing tight, and Cat could almost hear the coming tears.

Cat finished up with, "I'm very sorry for your loss. I didn't know Larry for long, but it was definitely a pleasure."

When she hung up, she didn't waste any time logging in. "I figure we'll work back through time."

"I agree," Duke answered.

"Do you want me to print it out for your use?"

"You'll need a mountain of paper for that. No, I can get the articles myself when I get home."

She turned to look at Duke. "His editor said he was a fine reporter and a fine human being."

Duke's face darkened slightly. "That's nice to hear. From Larry's telling, it sounded as if the newsroom could be a powder keg. Deadlines, ugly stories, sources that didn't call back. High pressure leading to short tempers, I guess."

Well, that was another thing to keep in mind, Cat thought. It might not have been the subject of one of his articles who wanted him dead. Maybe he had some enemies in the newsroom. "Do reporters make much in big cities?"

"Not from what I understand. It isn't poverty level, but it's not generous."

"That's what I thought." So how could another reporter afford to mount any kind of trip to kill Larry? And really, how bad could a newsroom explosion be? Bad enough to want to murder?

She expected to find more fertile ground in his investigative pieces.

"Oh man," she said as Larry's articles began popping up in a list of titles.

"What?"

She felt Duke lean closer.

"It looks like he did a lot of articles. This list is huge."

"He wrote a bunch of shorter pieces, like every other reporter. Partly because the paper wasn't going to pay him for a couple of years while he wasn't writing anything. Partly because newsrooms were shrinking—probably still are—and the workload went up for everyone. I gather he might have written a story or two every week."

"That's going to help," she said sarcastically. "I don't know how well these stories are tagged. Give me that one that upset you. Maybe that'll get us into something. Or maybe we need to read them all."

"That's quite a body of work. How long do we want to spend reading?"

She looked at him again, wondering if he expected her to let him be a second pair of eyes. The problem with that wasn't him reading Larry's articles—he had every right to—but he wouldn't see them through a cop's eyes.

Plus, she only had one computer. They'd have to read over each other's shoulders or take turns.

He spoke. "Well, the murder-for-hire story was in September, just over two years ago."

"Okay, I'll start there. Then maybe we should come forward in time before we start going backward. In case it was a more recent story."

She looked at the screen again. There'd be some eye-strain before long.

An hour later they headed for the truck stop to have lunch with Bud Wicke, the garage mechanic. The garage was conveniently located, in terms of his business. Bud sometimes had to run over to the truck stop to repair a long-haul truck, as well as performing routine repairs for locals.

As they drove toward the truck stop, Duke said, "Tell me a little about this guy, if you can. Just public knowledge."

Cat stifled a smile. "Like I could tell you much more than that."

"I know. Just the common knowledge."

"Well, Bud Wicke is one of our local garage mechanics. He started working for the place years ago and eventually bought it."

"Hard worker."

An insight. Cat hadn't really given it much thought. "I guess so. Anyway, I don't know much about him, because I've only been here a little over two years. Whether there's much more, I can't say. But I can still tell you he's a bit unexpected."

She felt Duke look at her. Amazing how you could tell when someone was watching you. "How so?" he asked.

"I hear he's got a college degree in math, as well as all his mechanic's certifications. Apparently, he just loves working on cars."

"He likes to learn."

"That would be my guess. Larry was interesting, too. He made friends with an eclectic group of people around here."

She turned into the truck stop parking lot and nosed toward a vacant parking space near the diner. On the far side of the lot there was parking for the big rigs, but that area was nearly full of idling trucks. Truckers preferred driving on nighttime roads if they had a choice, sleeping during the day to avoid heavy traffic. Hasty's diner stayed busy during much of the day.

Inside, the tables were busy. Hasty, a tall, lean man, flipped burgers on his grill and shuttled through breakfast orders and even veggies. He could do just about anything on that grill.

Bud Wicke sat at a corner table beside the wall of windows that surrounded the dining area on two sides. He smiled and waved them over.

Cat made the introductions, reminding Bud that

Duke was Larry's brother in case he'd forgotten or she had neglected to mention that the day before when she'd phoned him.

The waitress zoomed over with some menus, and both Bud and Duke immediately ordered coffee. Cat chose a diet cola.

Bud spoke after the waitress charged off with their orders. Breakfast for Duke, burgers for Bud and Cat, who felt she needed some recovery from all that Danish earlier.

"I'm so sorry," Bud said to Duke. "I liked Larry. He was a good man to play cards with and shoot the breeze over a few beers. He beat me at darts nearly every time I walked into Mahoney's. My ego was bruised." He said the last lightly, as if making fun of himself.

"I never wanted to face him in darts," Duke agreed. "Now, running—that was a whole different thing."

Cat spoke. "With you being a Ranger, I'm not surprised. Bet you could do more push-ups, too."

Duke laughed quietly. "I'm pretty sure."

"Larry mentioned you a couple of times," Bud offered. "He called you Duke."

"Everyone does."

Cat attempted a little humor. "Unless they call him *Major*."

That made a smile cross Bud's face. "Then I'll call you Duke. About Larry, I don't think I know anything useful. I was at the poker table and bar with him, but I sure as hell didn't see anything that would make me think he had enemies. Easy to get along with, always friendly. It must have been kids."

Although Bud didn't sound happy with that idea. He sounded like a man who would rather believe that than any alternative.

"So nothing about what he was here to work on?"

Bud shook his head. "I don't think I ever asked, either. He said once that he was here for the quiet to work on a book, but that was it. Oh yeah, he also said that he was a reporter."

Conversation lagged while they waited for lunch and started to eat. Cat's burger was perfectly cooked, juicy, the way she liked it.

She supposed that if she tried, she'd be able to ask a useful question, but she held back. It was important for Duke to ask the things he needed to know, certainly before she jumped in with any standard cop questions. Questions that Bud had probably answered right after the murder.

But suddenly she thought of something and asked anyway, mainly because Duke had fallen silent. "Did we interview you after the murder?"

Bud shook his head again. "Nobody came to me. Hardly matters, since after I heard about Larry, I tried to figure out if I knew anything, like him mentioning kids hanging around. If I'd thought of something, I'd have trotted over to your office. As it is…" He let it hang.

Then Bud straightened a bit, half a hamburger still in his hand. "I just remembered. Larry mentioned two days before he was killed that he felt watched sometimes. But he laughed it off, saying that anybody new around here would get watched. He was probably right."

Cat wasn't sure she agreed, and a glance at Duke suggested he wasn't buying it, either.

"Larry was good at laughing things off, including the threats he received as a reporter," Duke said.

"Threats? Seriously?" Bud looked appalled. "What was he reporting about? Major crime organizations? RICO violations?"

"In the past."

"Wow, I'm impressed. Every time I hear about something like that, I think the reporters must have a lot of guts." Then he shrugged. "Maybe it's in the family. You probably have a lot of guts, too, being a Ranger."

"I usually know where the threat is coming from. Larry would get these anonymous letters or emails. A few bothered him enough to turn over to the authorities, but most he just dismissed."

"Man. I liked the guy before, but now I'm feeling huge respect. I'd be looking over my damn shoulder every single minute."

"He wasn't, from what I saw of him. But his address? Under wraps."

"Understandable." Bud looked at the burger in his hand and put it down on the plate. "You think a threat might have followed him out here?"

"We don't know," Cat said swiftly, wanting to quash that rumor before it even got started. "But that's why we're asking if you heard anything about his work from Larry. To be sure."

"I get it." Bud's eyes darkened. "Makes more sense to me than some high school kids wanting his electronics."

Cat answered him. "Keep that under your hat, please. It's only a remote possibility."

At that, Bud's face relaxed. "I thought it was strange that Larry would come to the back of beyond just to write a book, but the idea that someone followed him out here? Even wilder."

Cat couldn't disagree. It *did* seem wild, and very unlikely. Chances were, Larry hadn't even told anyone where he was going. But no matter where he'd gone, he'd have received cell phone messages. Only law enforcement agencies could have tracked him, and there was no evidence for that.

Duke insisted on picking up the entire tab. Bud left, promising he'd think more about it, but Cat didn't expect anything.

"He played close to the vest, all right," she said to Duke as they walked back to the car.

"That's Larry. Damn it."

"The ultimate proof is that Ben didn't have any idea, either. Imagine not telling your significant other even the least little thing about what you were working on."

"Imagine not telling your brother you were about to wreck his career."

She looked at him over the roof of the car. "Do you think he could have known that?"

Once again, she watched him stare into the distance as he thought. It was as if he'd learned long ago that answers might not be right under his nose. A trained response?

He shook his head a bit, then folded himself into her car. She followed suit and turned over the ignition.

"He may not have known," Duke said as she steered them out of the lot. "But he might have ticked someone off farther up the chain of command."

"No way to know anything about this case," she remarked sourly. "God, I hate this. Usually there's a link to someone or to an event that gives us direction. We've got no direction here. We need someone to spill a few beans."

"Good luck with that."

It often proved to be exactly that kind of luck that nailed a criminal. For some reason she would never understand, people seemed to need to talk or brag about what they'd done.

Duke was disappointed, even though he'd admitted yesterday that his original plan had deflated. She wondered if she should set up meetings with the other five poker buddies anyway. Just to settle Duke's mind. Although at this point, if he thought it was a waste, he wouldn't want to pursue it any further.

Like Bud, she wasn't buying the teenage home-invasion theory. She'd had trouble with it since she'd discovered Larry's body. Too savage, too brutal to be kids who just wanted to steal. It would have been much easier for them to hightail it.

"You know," she said to Duke as they pulled into her driveway, "it would not be smart for us to start following a single theory about Larry's murder. It could blind us to something important."

"I agree." But that was all he said as he followed her into the house.

Now they were faced with reading more of his brother's

articles. Or at least the stories that seemed as if they could have lit a fire somewhere.

Like the one about murder for hire in the Army. That was the most recent investigative piece, and considering what had been happening to Duke, someone had been disturbed. Maybe more than disturbed.

Then she remembered Duke's reaction when he learned the crime scenes were too clean. "Did Larry ever write about corrupt cops?"

"I don't know. Like I said, I didn't read everything he wrote, even the big stories. He rarely mentioned them to me, so basically I never thought about it."

Thus, it appeared, they were going to wade through the work product of a very prolific man.

"I can't imagine being a reporter and having to write on such tight deadlines."

Duke followed her down the hall. "Larry seemed to thrive on them."

"He'd have to."

EVENING WAS SETTLING in with dim light, and once again the colder temperatures settled in with it. Spring around here could even mean snowstorms, but right now Cat thought she detected dry air with the cold.

Duke took himself out for a run. She watched him leave, loping easily. She wished she could find such a comfortable pace while running.

Then she headed for her refrigerator to see if she could rustle up something for dinner for the two of them. She didn't think Duke was going to want to stop reading after a meal. *Dog with a bone*, she thought, not for the first time.

He might even want to stay up all night. She wouldn't be able to blame him, but she groaned inwardly anyway. Lack of sleep never made any investigation easier. She'd had to do it plenty of times, but when the brain got tired, so did its thinking.

Of course, she hadn't been out to shop for two. Her fridge stared back at her with little that would stretch that far. She headed for the cupboard that served as her pantry and started scoping out the other foods.

All of which was a distraction from thinking about how dead in the water this case had grown.

Nothing in the fridge, nothing in the cupboard and nothing in the file.

Remembering the Hodgeses, she called. Mark Hodges was willing to meet with Duke. As an instructor at the junior college, he had a more convenient schedule for setting up an interview. His wife, Marjory, taught kindergarten, however.

"I don't think she could manage meeting Duke until tomorrow night," Mark said. "Will that do?"

"Absolutely. I appreciate this," Cat replied.

Mark Hodges sighed audibly. "Some of the questions from the cops who came to investigate made me uneasy."

Cat instantly grew alert. "How so?"

"Well…" He hesitated. "Frankly, I wondered if they were trying to connect it to the murder last week. It's not anything they said, but a feeling I got. It bothered me because of what happened to Larry Duke. Are Marjory and I alive only because we were out of town?"

Cat wanted to reassure him and sought a way to do so without denying what might be true, however remotely. "I don't think it's likely, Mark. I mean, the two crimes probably aren't related to begin with. Otherwise, from what I read in the file, they aren't at all similar in terms of the burglaries."

The last part wasn't exactly true. The fact that both scenes seemed to be clean of physical evidence seriously gnawed at her. But Mark sounded relieved, and that was what mattered.

After she hung up, she thought about dinner again, then just shrugged it away. She didn't have anything to cook other than eggs and toast, she didn't really feel like cooking, and if Duke was hungry, she could bring out the peanut butter, jam and bread.

She might be a woman, but that didn't make her responsible to cook for him. Heck, he wasn't even a guest so much as a necessary invitee.

Satisfied, she resisted the urge to go to the computer again because he'd just want to go over it all again. She doubted he'd be happy with *her* deciding what was important.

And my, wasn't she working herself into an absolute tear of a mood?

"Aagh," she said to the empty room, then settled in to wait for Duke. At this rate, she was going to want action as much as Duke. She wondered if he was exacerbating her impatience.

Go exercise, she told herself. She had the time.

WHILE DUKE WAS pounding the pavement and Cat was pounding her treadmill, the three men out in the gorge huddled around a fire.

"I'm not used to this cold anymore," the third man said. "I know it was worse in the 'Stan, but I'm feeling the freaking cold *now*." Grousing came with the territory.

"It's not the cold that's getting to me," said the second man. "I am so sick of being stuck. We've got to get this laptop charged. We've got to find a way to get Major His Mightiness Duke out of the way."

"Seriously?" The first man was past being patient. He was growing angry, maybe because of the way they were stuck. "Getting rid of Duke might be the stupidest thing we've done yet even if we want to. Scrub it from your brain cells."

"He's slowing us down."

"Bull!" said the first man. "We're stuck because we found out that Larry Duke might have passed data to someone for safekeeping. We've already made what may have been a wasted break-in, because we didn't know exactly what we were looking for. *I'll* decide about him."

The other two exchanged looks, wondering again if Man One might have a stake in this beyond money.

"Yeah, yeah," muttered the second man. "I gotta recharge this laptop and cell. How in the name of whatever am I supposed to do that?"

"You could just go into town and do it," said the third man.

"Oh, for…" said the second. "Haven't we been trying

to avoid being seen? Place this small, someone would notice and remember."

"Yup," said the first man. "I'm getting tired of sitting on our butts stuck, just like y'all. But I've also been trying to figure out what kind of diversion would get that cop away from Larry's house, and what kind of surveillance we should do on another target around here."

"But we don't know what we're looking for," argued the third man, sounding just a bit whiny.

"Exactly," the first man agreed. "Exactly. I'm thinking about driving into town."

Silence greeted his words initially. Then the second man waved his hand.

"Hello?" he said. "We discussed this. No town."

A snicker escaped the third man. The first man let it pass.

Instead of responding directly, he said, "I've got to figure out a disguise. Then, after we get some intel, we can act."

"What intel?" the second man demanded.

"To find out more people that Larry Duke interacted with. More hiding places to look. I can probably do a recharge there. Enough waiting for the cop to disappear. It'd be better if no one broke into that house while we're still here."

He looked at each of them individually. "I'll figure this out, because you're not the only ones tired of spinning your wheels. Damn messed-up operation. I'm going to have to fix it somehow. And if I decide Major Duke has the info, I'm going to send him to the next world."

The other two didn't doubt he would.

Chapter Eight

Cat was waiting for Duke when he returned. He carried two large paper bags into the kitchen.

"I got us some dinner," he said. "And I hope it's okay that I parked my rental on the street."

She noticed his hair was still damp. "Thank you, the parking is okay, and how about we change the terms of this arrangement?"

He turned from putting the bags on the counter to look at her. "How so?"

"Just check out of the motel and bring your stuff over here. This is ridiculous. As near as I can tell, you're using the motel only for clothing storage and showers. Well, I've got the room for your clothes, and I've got a working shower."

He hesitated visibly. "I'm intruding too much on you."

"Really? This would be more convenient. Just get your damn stuff and move in. I can spare the room. I even have a washer and dryer that I hereby permit you to use."

At that, a twinkle appeared in his eyes. "You sure?"

"I sound sure, don't I? Or maybe I wasn't emphatic enough."

"You were," he allowed. "Okay, I'll move in. Now, dinner? Maude was making some fried chicken. I hope you like it."

"I think I'd like anything that came out of that woman's kitchen."

He smiled. "Good, because the deed is done."

HE GOT THE dishes for them, then spread the food out on the kitchen table.

"You know," she said, "you don't have to keep buying meals for us."

"Sure I do." He passed her a stack of napkins. "I don't want you cooking for me, and my cooking skills are limited. When you live a military life as a single guy, you get used to chow halls and restaurants. Or in the field you heat up rations. I have a kitchenette in my quarters, but it doesn't see much use."

"I didn't feel like cooking," she admitted.

"I don't blame you. And if you feel like you need to cook for me, stop. That's not your job. Hell, you don't have to be polite, either. I've moved in on you."

"At my invitation."

He sat across from her again. *His* chair now, she supposed. He spent enough time in it. Not that she had a problem.

While they ate Maude's fried chicken and her homemade potato salad, they chatted casually.

"You were lucky to get the potato salad," she remarked.

"Really? Why?"

"Maude only makes it once in a while, because it's

time-consuming. When I complimented it one time, she groused, asking me if I had any idea how long it took to peel that many potatoes. Point taken."

He chuckled. "Never having made it, I don't know."

"I've made it, but once I imagined how many potatoes she'd have to peel and turn into cubes, and slices of celery she'd have to clean and chop…never mind the quantity of eggs and onions…" Cat shrugged. "I got it. Four servings is one thing. A ton for all her customers who want to eat it? A whole other game."

"I like Maude. She reminds me of more than a few drill instructors."

She had to grin. Having only seen them in movies, Cat could easily see Maude in that role.

Holding a piece of half-gnawed chicken leg, Cat was the first to dive into the interrupted conversation about the case. "I'm getting as impatient with all this as you are. I know better, but frustration is making me want to erupt."

Duke nodded. "I understand."

"I bet you do. In fact, I know you do."

"I'm that transparent, huh?"

"Maybe. It's not like you're trying to conceal it. Or are you?"

"Nah. It's an evident fact. I kind of announced it when I got here. You think of anything?"

Cat wondered how much she should wade into the morass in her mind right now. She didn't want her feelings to ratchet his up. On the other hand…

"Duke? What you said about the crime scenes being

clean. I've been thinking about that, too. It bothers me. I mean..."

"Yes?"

Cat looked toward her kitchen windows over the sink. Dark outside now, she could see the reflection of the kitchen in them. Time to close the curtains, but she didn't move.

"What bothers you?" he asked.

She sighed. "Since I read the reports, I've been telling myself that people have learned a lot from TV and movies about evidence at crime scenes. Sometimes that doesn't mean a whole lot, but sometimes it could. If you start by wearing gloves and a hat over all your hair, then there's a whole lot less to worry about. Most people probably get that much. But what else is common knowledge? And if the knowledge isn't common, then you have to wonder who knows it."

"You're right. Eat, Cat. You didn't finish your burger earlier. So where is this leading you?"

"I wish I knew. But it certainly mitigates against teens, don't you think? Even knowing this stuff, they might not think of it in the rush of the moment. I'd actually expect them to be disorganized."

"I hear you."

Loud and clear, she thought. His tension had increased slightly since she brought it up. "I have some good news, though. The Hodgeses will see us tomorrow evening. I hope you can wait that long."

"I'll have to, won't I?"

"Uh, yeah. Anyway, I don't know what you expect to find that the techs didn't come across."

"I don't know. I want details, of course. I want to look around. I want their impressions, not a list of missing items."

"Okay. We'll see if it helps any."

She resumed eating her chicken and potato salad, deciding she should let him lead the conversation. At this point she was willing to look in any direction for a useful tidbit.

"Were you born here?"

The question surprised her, seeming to come out of left field. "No. My mom moved here to take a teaching job at the college. I visited a few times before I moved here to take care of her."

"She was sick?"

"Terminal cancer. At least I could help."

"That's a tall task. I hear it wears people out emotionally."

"I don't know. She was the only thing on my mind. I didn't have anything else to worry about. Anyway, I stayed on after her death because Gage offered me a job."

He nodded, then pushed his plate to one side. "You were in law enforcement before, right?"

"Yes. Which is why I'm hating this whole situation right now. I know from experience how frustrating cases like this can be, but that doesn't mean I like it."

Duke surprised her by reaching across the table to gently grip her forearm. It was a brief touch, but it sent her mind careening in a different direction. Right then, she'd have been happy to forget the case and focus instead on the warm honey he'd sent running through her veins. On the even more pleasant tingle she felt between her thighs.

God, bad timing. She wrestled herself back into line. "I understand that a lot of this job is sedentary. Paper trails, reading about evidence, making phone calls. Hoping that someone will spill the beans to someone else. Looking for bad relationships. An investigator needs to depend on a lot of other people, too. But no matter how many times I experience it, I will never like it when a trail goes cold."

"I can imagine."

She believed he did. Being stalled was never pleasant in any part of life. He was a person of action by trade. She was beginning to believe she was one, too.

"I'm impressed," he said, "that you dropped everything to come here and take care of your mother."

A diversion. Maybe she needed it. "It's what you do for someone you love."

A simple answer, straight to the point. It had never occurred to her to do anything else.

When they finished eating, she put the leftovers in her refrigerator while he put the dishes in her dishwasher. "There should be enough chicken and potato salad for lunch tomorrow."

"That was the plan."

Then they returned to her office and their reading. Sitting there, scanning articles without apparent end, didn't satisfy her. But no piece of evidence, no clue, was too small to consider. The downside of the job.

It was nearly midnight when they headed to their

separate beds. For the very first time it occurred to her that she might prefer Duke beside her.

Oh, for Pete's sake, Cat. Straighten up and fly right.

DUKE STOOD AT the window in Cat's office. He'd opened the curtains to let the night in, having turned off all the lights.

He liked the night. While threats often worsened in the dark, he knew darkness also offered him protection. An opportunity to move surreptitiously. A way to conceal himself from the enemy or prying eyes.

Stealth was part of his job at times, and he knew its importance. He thought about the two crime scenes, about why no one had heard a break-in. Stealth. That was leading him down a path he didn't want to follow.

The three soldiers mentioned in Larry's extensive article had been charged. But someone must have paid them for those killings. Hired them. He'd assumed it might have been one of the warlords in Afghanistan, since no other charges had emerged.

Even if it had been a warlord, that could have caused ripples up the chain of command. It wouldn't be the first time commanding officers had gotten into trouble just for not being aware of what their soldiers were up to. For failing to control their men. For failing in their duty, which Duke sometimes thought required psychic talents or prescience.

But usually it didn't. Usually there was a whisper in the wind to alert officers that something below them was going seriously wrong.

The attack on Duke's career could have been as simple as that. Or it could have been based on the faulty assumption that Duke had been one of Larry's sources. Damned for breaking the code of silence.

Or to put it in the vernacular, *don't be a rat*.

Thinking Duke was a rat could have put some officers on a mission to ease him out of the officer corps.

But it could have been something far, far worse. As in someone in uniform had paid those soldiers to kill. Or someone in uniform had sold his soul to a faction. To a warlord or a politician.

He really needed to read Larry's article in detail, to look for a clue in his brother's writing that might tell him which it had been. But maybe Larry hadn't known how far up the tree this sludge went. And maybe someone thought he knew and was preparing to write a book about it. Or maybe that had been exactly what Larry was doing. Maybe he *had* known.

Too many maybes. Way too many.

He placed his hands on the window frame and leaned forward, feeling the muscles in his back and shoulders stretch. He needed that stretching. The tension there was building into a headache.

His thoughts drifted to Cat. He understood her impatience, even understood why she stuck with a job that often frustrated her. It was the challenge of the chase, the victory when a case was solved.

He was developing a serious admiration for her. She wasn't a quitter, not in any sense of the word. Imagine her caring for her mother that way. Determination and love, an awesome combination. Her job was difficult and frustrating, but she still did it. She believed in justice, too, just like Larry.

He was sure his presence was increasing the pressure on her. Sure, she wanted to solve the case for her own satisfaction, but now she had to deal with him wanting a solution for personal reasons.

Not that he thought she didn't care about the collateral victims in a crime of this nature. She'd said enough for him to know she wasn't a machine, that she did care about a victim's family and friends. But still, having him in her face every day must be uncomfortable.

He sighed and leaned away from the window a dozen times, stretching even more, modified push-ups.

She was an attractive woman, and this setup wasn't helping him to ignore it. The urge to explore her, to bury himself in her, was growing. He knew he just wanted to forget for a few hours, and that wasn't fair to her.

Or maybe the desire was more than that, but he didn't want to chance it as long as there was a question in his own mind about why he felt it.

Apart from his attraction to her, he liked her. Really liked her. He knew she was handling him, but except for that one minor confrontation in front of the department store, she'd managed him deftly.

Yup. She considered his feelings, fed him what she could to make him feel better about his part in this. She was measured when she could have exploded. She shared that she was frustrated, too, essentially telling him that he wasn't alone in this madness that had overtaken him.

And it was madness. He wasn't a man to go off half-cocked with a stupid plan. The fact that he had burst into her life making unreasonable demands, yet she'd treated him with such care...

A remarkable woman, a remarkable law officer. She, and her boss, could have kicked him to the curb and told him to stay in his own lane. He'd have been floundering, no matter how much he had initially tried to believe that he'd find *something*. Instead, between them, they'd thrown him a lifeline. Even though she clearly hadn't wanted to be his keeper, she'd shouldered the job.

He pushed away from the window one last time, then dropped to the narrow space between her desk and the bed and began to perform one-armed push-ups.

Exercise. It helped most things, most especially directionless tension. It wasn't as if he could jog out into the night and solve his brother's murder.

"Damn it, Larry," he said into the darkness. "Couldn't you have confided in just *one* person?"

But the person he might, just might, have confided in had already turned his back.

The guilt had become insurmountable. Larry couldn't forgive him now.

Justice. Larry cried out for it. It had been his guiding light.

It had become one for Duke as well.

Morning couldn't come soon enough.

Chapter Nine

In the morning, Cat found her sleepy way into the kitchen and started coffee. A quick scan of her fridge—which looked awfully familiar after her hunt last evening—revealed enough eggs to scramble for two. A reasonably fresh loaf of rye bread also sat on the counter.

Eggs, toast and jam this morning, she thought as she yawned. Or peanut butter on the toast. She always liked that, and it helped keep her full until lunch.

She was still yawning when Duke appeared. He had dark circles under his eyes, announcing the kind of night he'd had. He rounded the table to get himself some coffee then nearly sagged into his chair.

"Bad night?" she asked before yawning yet again.

"Yeah." He offered no additional information. Not that she really needed any.

"I was thinking," he said.

She felt there was more to that. "About what?"

"I'll talk once I have coherent thoughts."

Eventually she felt her stomach rumble and rose to make toast for them. "Raspberry jam?" she asked. "Or plain toast or…"

A small laugh escaped him. "Whatever you're having, if you don't mind."

She didn't mind. Facing another day of reading Larry's articles didn't appeal to her. Necessary, but no fun. Larry had been a great writer, but news story after news story wasn't exactly gripping.

They took a couple of brisk walks during the day to work out the kinks. Running into Edith Jasper, who was walking her harlequin Great Dane, Cat and Duke stopped to talk to her for a few minutes.

Edith was upbeat as always. "Bailey keeps me in shape," she said when Duke admired him. "He's not going to settle for a trip around the backyard."

Duke flashed a smile. "He's a big guy."

"Folks tell me he's too big for me, but I've had him for four years, and he's never once been a problem. Doesn't tug hard, doesn't run into me when he's exuberant. Nope, he's a good boy. Aren't you, Bailey?"

Bailey's tail wagged happily.

Then Edith zeroed in on Duke. "You're Larry Duke's brother, right? I never met him but, on this town's endless grapevine, I heard he was a good guy. Friendly and fun. I'm sorry this happened."

"I guess my identity is running around on that grapevine," Duke said as he and Cat continued their walk.

"I'd be surprised if it wasn't. You're a stranger with an interesting backstory. Maybe I should have asked how much information was making the rounds."

He swiveled his head to look at her. "Worried about it?"

"Only where the information might have come from."

Back at her house, their legs comfortably stretched

and unknotted from walking, they ate leftover fried chicken, then settled in once again at her computer.

Cat wished she had a second screen. So much more comfortable for them both if Duke didn't have to read over her shoulder.

Then she noticed something. "You've come back to that military exposé several times. What's bugging you? Was that what you were thinking about this morning?"

"I keep trying to glean something more from it," Duke admitted.

"But you think it might be more of a problem than his older stories?" She swiveled her chair around so she could see him directly.

"I'm wondering."

"Because of what someone has done to your career?"

"Not entirely." He paused and rubbed his chin. "Sure, they could think I was a source for Larry's article. Even though I had nothing to do with those guys. Didn't even know they existed until Larry's story was published."

"They're not Rangers like you?"

"Nope. Regular troops, a few tours in Afghanistan."

"So what else do you think might be going on?" She had to keep from leaning forward in anticipation. She could feel the first little bursts of excitement that he might be providing a new angle.

"Well, somebody had to pay these guys enough to do the killing. Three that were evidently enticed into this operation. Now, people at their rank don't make a lot of money, but you'd still have to pay for their silence so they wouldn't brag about what they were doing."

He was probably right about that. "Go on," Cat said.

"Anyway, given that someone was paying them, the question becomes who. Officers receive decent pay, but enough to hire hit men? I don't think so, unless these guys were very cheap. Which could happen."

"You just don't think it's likely."

He shrugged. "I also wouldn't have thought that a person or persons would try to kill my career over something Larry wrote. Sure, rats are hated, but it also suggests that someone is seriously scared." He raised his arm and started drumming his fingers on the end of her desk.

"I don't have a link to anyone, obviously," he continued. "I may be all wet. But I started thinking about someone selling out to a warlord. There'd be a lot of money in that for whoever was directing this from above. Someone *had* to be. It's not as if these guys could just wander off for a night to kill someone. Wandering off gets you in trouble. So, it seems to me that someone was paying them, and someone ensured they weren't on duty at those times."

"Wait," Cat said. "Clarify, please. I take it you can't just call in sick and miss a day?"

"Nope. You have to go on sick call, seeking to get treatment of some kind. Get a duty excuse. If you're in a forward operating base or something like that, disappearing for even a few hours could get you charged for being absent without leave."

"Wow. That's a restrictive environment."

He shook his head. "For good reason. You see that in a lot of jobs in civilian life, too." Duke half laughed.

"If you take time off without permission, you're stealing from the Army."

"Seriously?"

"Seriously. Uncle Sam owns you, the Army pays you. Hell, you can get in trouble for a bad sunburn, because you should have avoided it. Damaging government property, or something like it."

Cat remembered her own experience. "A long time ago, I worked with a guy who got fired for claiming jury duty for the second time in two weeks. The company found out when the police called wanting to know if he was on sick time or something. Well, the woman who answered the phones put two and two together. And as it happens, he didn't take sick time but put in the hours on his time sheet as being on jury duty, which meant he got paid his full wages for eight hours. Not once, but twice."

"I'm not surprised he got fired. Pretty much the same for a soldier. Although since you can't be fired, you get other consequences. Anyway, point remains, these guys had someone up the chain covering for them."

She rested her elbow on the arm of her chair and considered this new perspective. It was sure an interesting one. "But would some officer send someone this far to take out your brother? See, that's the part I'm having a little trouble with. Why would anyone at this late date want to take Larry out? He'd already done his worst."

"Maybe. That's part of what's bothering me, too. So many uncertainties. Fact is, however, if several people up the chain have reason to be concerned, yeah, they could send someone out here. For heaven's sake, they got three guys to engage in killing for hire. Why wouldn't they be able to hire some guy to put paid to Larry?"

"Do you think that's what he was writing a book about?"

"I don't know, obviously, and neither do they. Every way I look at it, I keep wondering who could do this and why. Yeah, years back he made some very public links between domestic terrorism groups, and heads rolled. He was involved in a RICO investigation that sent some people to jail. The question is, who would come after him because he was writing a book?"

"I wish we knew if it was even that." She glanced at her computer and was startled by the time. "I need to figure out dinner."

"No, you don't. I'll run out and get us something. Any preferences?"

"There's the supermarket subs. At least they have veggies on them."

His eyes crinkled at the corner. "And a whole lot less fat."

She didn't even hesitate. "I'll ride along, if that's okay. I need some stuff anyway."

"You're on."

And at least it was out of the house. At this rate she could get cabin fever.

THE THREE MEN gathered around their paltry fire again as twilight blanketed the land. The minute the sun went behind the mountains, the temperature dropped quickly.

The first man opened his rucksack and pulled out

Larry Duke's computer and cell phone. "Charged," he announced.

Man Two looked delighted, but the third guy was still feeling annoyed. "You get seen?"

"Of course."

"What the hell? You weren't even disguised."

The first man just shrugged. "You ever been to a truck stop? The place is crawling with people who don't live around here. Even the locals wouldn't notice a new face in that crowd."

"Oh." Man Three grew subdued.

"I was wondering if I could gather much intelligence, though. I knew if I started asking questions, it'd be noticed. Especially questions about Larry Duke. So I just listened." He picked up a twig and snapped it, then threw it on the fire. One of the other guys had started the coffee.

"Did you at least get to eat real food?" the second man asked almost wistfully.

"I was in a truck stop diner." As if that answered the question. Which it did, however indirectly.

"So what now?" asked the third man.

The first man pointed at the second. "You spend tonight hacking your way into the computer and the phone. Hack as hard as you ever have." He indicated the third guy. "We're going for another break-in tonight."

"Is the house empty?"

"No. Plan on being silent. Completely silent. Guy is single, lives alone, owns a food store."

"How'd you find out about him?"

For once, Man One looked a little less angry. "Someone mentioned Major Duke. They were behind me while I ate, and he was curious about why Duke's talking to certain people. We start there. After that we've got a tougher problem. A guy who owns an auto repair in town. He was mentioned, too, and doesn't live alone."

It grew quiet for a while, the only noticeable sound the night wind blowing through surrounding growth. Spring was trying to emerge on this sparse land.

"Anything else?" the third man asked eventually.

"Only Duke."

"We're going to have to take him out," said the second man.

"We shouldn't, much as I'd like to," the first man said. "We're hardly covert if we do that. It's not enough that he's nosing around with the help of that damn deputy."

"He is?" The second man sat up straighter.

"That's what I'm gathering, little as it is. It's thin intel, but I'm going to assume my conclusions are true. Safest thing to do."

The gloom was deepening, both in the outside world and among the men. What had looked like a relatively easy mission had descended steadily into a chaotic mess. They'd seen that on the battlefield, but they hadn't expected it here.

"I hope," said the second man, "that this crap is as important as someone seems to think."

"I hope," said the third guy, "that you want the money enough to shut up and do whatever's necessary."

"Hell, yeah," said the second man. "But who's taking the risk out here?"

Good question. But it was always that way. The grunts did the real work while too many of the candy-ass brass sat at computers and desks.

The first man poured himself coffee in the collapsible tin cup he carried nearly everywhere. It would cool down soon, but at least it was real coffee.

"Thing is," he said, "if I was sure the only person involved back there is the one who hired us, I might kill *him*. But I don't know that there aren't others."

"Too bad how much we don't know," muttered the second guy.

"I don't think whoever he is knew. I think he thought we'd get to Larry Duke and that would be the end of it. I got the impression he's not happy that we had to kill Duke. Not at all. It's a mess, all right."

But there was no point in beating that horse to death. They all agreed on that, so silence returned as they listened to the wind whisper.

THE HODGESES HAD been nice. They let Duke and Cat inside, showed them the scene and explained in detail everything that was missing. From a wide-screen TV to a computer, electronics appeared to have been the target.

What had interested Cat most was Duke's prowl outside the Hodges house. He'd studied the privacy-fenced backyard, the door that had been jimmied, the bottom edges of windows that had not. He'd been interested in looking through those windows, too.

"Did you learn anything?" she asked as they walked home.

"I may have. Can't be sure."

"Quit being inscrutable and share."

Mark Hodges's only connection with Larry had been playing darts with him a few times at Mahoney's. On the surface this robbery didn't appear to be related in any way to Larry's murder.

On the surface. She wondered if, during his inspection of the property, Duke had noticed something that other eyes might have missed.

"Let's go to Mahoney's," he said. "If you don't mind. When we went there together, I got the feeling a few of those guys wanted to talk to me."

"I got the same feeling. Let's go."

Mahoney's was in full swing for a weeknight. Not as packed as on a weekend but packed enough. Laughter had grown louder as the beer did its work. Two guys played darts; another four gathered around the pool table in the back room. Friendly enjoyment permeated the place.

This time Duke took a table. Cat noticed that he maneuvered himself in a way that kept his back against a wall. Interesting.

Duke went over to the bar and snagged a longneck for Cat and a draft for himself. It wasn't long after he sat again that a man came over to him and shook his hand before accepting an invitation to sit with them. Duke didn't move, his chair still positioned to keep his back to the wall.

"I'm Frank Ludlow," the guy said. "I enjoyed Larry's company. You never saw anyone get accepted around here as fast as he did. People barely met him before they liked him and decided he was okay."

Duke spoke. "A talent for a journalist, to be able to do that."

"Well, he seemed to do it naturally. You never got the feeling it was an act."

"It wasn't. That was just Larry."

Frank nodded. "That I can believe. He sure livened this place up. Not that it's ever dull, but when he'd play darts with some of us, he gathered a whole group to watch. He could always tell a good joke or a good story. Everyone was glad to see him walk in."

"Did he ever mention what he was working on?"

"A book. That seemed reasonable, given that he was a reporter. I don't think anyone asked more about it."

Cat spoke. "Did he ever seem to be questioning anyone?"

"If he was, no one mentioned it. Why? You think that could be a clue?"

"I don't know," Cat admitted. "I'm looking everywhere and anywhere that might help."

"I can help," Frank said. "I'll ask around, see if anyone noticed anything. I'll let you know."

That was a step in the right direction. It sometimes amazed her how much people knew that they didn't realize they knew. Little things, occasionally very useful.

"Mind if we stay for a second beer?" Duke asked her.

"Not at all. That may have been productive. If someone else wants to meet you, I'm up for it."

After a little while, he went to get more beer for them. He also came back with a bowl of nuts to share.

When he settled again, she noted the restless roving of his eyes, as if he were trying to take in every little detail. Or maybe to memorize faces. She could have asked him, but she didn't. It just didn't seem important enough.

"Did something grab you at the Hodges place?"

His gaze snapped back to her. "Only that it was an easy place to rob. Big privacy fence, windows low enough to peer into rooms, a door latch that could have been opened with a credit card. Not exactly much security."

"Not something you need a whole lot of around here. Is that important?"

"I'm not sure. I mean, it was easy enough to get in there unseen, so that argues for kids again. Or it just may have been easy."

She curved one corner of her mouth. "All that uncertainty you mentioned."

"It sure didn't clarify the matter. It wouldn't have required any real skill to carry that burglary off."

"Anything else?"

"Actually, yeah. The idea that Larry's story might have triggered someone in the Army? I could be targeted, too."

Shock rippled through her, icy and electric. "But no one could know you were coming out here."

"Really?" He arched a brow. "I took leave. Who wouldn't have guessed that I was going to show up here right after my brother was murdered? Only someone who didn't know we were brothers."

"But…"

"What if I'm the rat they suspect?"

Cat settled back in her chair, turning the cold bottle in her hands, feeling stupid for not having put that together herself. "Damn, Duke."

"Yeah."

She looked up from the bottle, noticed he had leaned forward, surrounding his draft glass with powerful forearms. "Is that why your back is against the wall?"

"You noticed."

"I'm not completely dumb. Yeah, I noticed."

"I don't think you're dumb at all. Why would you think so?"

Cat sighed. "Because I didn't make the connection you just did. It's not like you didn't give me all the pieces."

"Maybe I assembled them differently. I'm used to having to consider things in terms of threat. No reason you should be."

"It's my job, in a way."

"No, getting a solution is your job. Not planning for off-the-wall threats."

Duke had a point. She sipped more of her beer, seeing the bar in a different light. He hadn't just been taking mental snapshots. Maybe he was looking for something out of place.

She looked around, really looked, for the first time. "I know all these people. Regulars."

"Thanks for telling me."

She hoped he could relax a bit with that information. Not that she was sure she'd ever seen him truly relaxed. All she knew was that he sometimes seemed less tense.

A couple of other patrons came over to shake his hand and express their sympathy, but neither of them knew Larry, or even what he'd been working on.

"I hope Frank can find out something," Cat said later, while they walked home.

Agreement seemed to radiate from him.

That night, for the first time, she checked all the windows and doors to make sure they were locked. Remembering what he had said about looking into windows, she closed all the curtains. Then she considered upgrading her locks the next day.

She didn't like the feeling. She'd gotten used to the mostly bucolic life around here. Yeah, bad things happened, but usually on such a limited scale that folks around here didn't live in constant fear.

That might be changing for her, for a while.

ALONE ONCE AGAIN in his bedroom, Duke stared out at the night. It was possible that someone was watching him right now. Standing out there in the dark, out of sight, eyes on.

He didn't feel watched, however, and he had a deep trust for that instinct. It had served him well more times than he could remember.

He remembered Cat's reaction to him saying he might be a target. She shouldn't have felt stupid for not thinking of it. He hadn't exactly leaped to the conclusion himself. It sounded a little weird when he said it out loud. Over-the-top.

But given what had happened, and his suspicions, it really *wasn't* over-the-top. Not at all. He knew the kind of people he was dealing with, what they might consider doing to protect their careers and their reputations.

A few men went to war and came back killers. Even

developed a taste for it. Most had a harder time with guilt and memory.

As a man had once said, "War is an atrocity-making situation."

Hell, yeah. Dealing with it afterward was rarely easy.

But then there were those who liked it. Psychopaths, or whatever they were called these days.

Regardless, if war unleashed psychopaths, then there were psychopaths inside the command structure. Someone who'd be willing to order Larry killed. Someone who'd be willing to order Duke's death. Someone who wouldn't care but felt he'd gain from it.

Hell. He pulled the curtains closed. He wanted to escape this obsession for a little while. He considered taking a long run, then decided against it. He needed distraction, not the rush of endorphins through his system.

Leaving the bedroom, he padded down the hall in his stocking feet, which felt exposed to him. *Boots on* was every infantryman's rule. Boots could help you run over dangerous ground and protect your feet.

But walking around in boots might disturb Cat, and he didn't want to do that.

In the kitchen, he started coffee. Checking the bakery bag on the counter, he found more Danish. Probably a little stale by now, but still edible. He placed one on a plate, then joined it with steaming coffee. Such luxuries.

Now that his initial shock was passing, memories of Larry were resurfacing. They were all good memories, and they could still make him smile. Even when his chest ached so bad he thought he might not be able to draw another breath. God, it hurt.

He knew he was trying to avoid it, but this grief was apt to kill him. Larry had been an essential part of his life even when distance and time had separated them.

He felt as if he was about to bury half of himself. The best part. And he knew he was going to miss Larry's voice and grin forever.

Sunny days playing baseball. Long, lazy summers during school breaks when Mom had always promised they were going to do exciting things. Inevitably, the planned day trips didn't last long, whether because she quickly wore out or the budget wouldn't support it. It didn't matter to either him or Larry.

Instead they'd had the hills near the house. Trees to climb in, forts to build, fish to catch and a river to swim in. In the winter, endless hours were spent skating on the frozen river and trying to master the art of building an igloo or playing hockey with friends.

Duke heard a sound and twisted to see Cat shuffling into the kitchen. She wore a bright blue terry-cloth robe over pajamas.

"Did I wake you?" he immediately asked.

"You might have if I'd been asleep."

"You, too?"

"Some nights are harder than others." She poured herself coffee, then peeked into the pastry bag. "You want this?"

"Help yourself. Just a little stale."

"A shame to let that happen to Melinda's baking."

Coffee and Danish in hand, she returned to the table. "What's keeping you up?"

"I was just thinking about Larry. Memories of good times."

Cat smiled at him, a soft expression. He liked it when she smiled, but this one was special somehow. Like a warm connection.

"Care to share?" she asked.

"Not sure what to tell you. I'm kind of having a collage of memories—golden moments, if you will. Snapshots. We were close, almost like twins."

"God, that must hurt."

"It does." No point minimizing it. Since she'd joined him, the steel band around his chest had loosened a bit, but it was still there, restricting his breathing.

He continued, thinking she might like to hear a little about Larry the kid. She'd known him, after all. "We were best buddies all the way up until we separated for college. Me to the military academy, him to another college."

"Wait," she interrupted. "You went to West Point?"

"Sure did."

Wow, she thought, impressed. Then, "I'm sorry I interrupted your memories of Larry."

"No problem. They're coming as they come. Like a river that's determined to flow, but not always rapidly. Tonight, like I said, it's random snapshots. A hazy recollection of golden days. I don't know about your childhood, but ours was mostly great. Having Larry there made it even better."

"A built-in playmate."

"You bet. Best friend. We liked to camp in the backyard when we were in elementary school. It was like a huge adventure to be out there alone in a tent with night all around. We loved the flashlights. I bet our parents got sick of buying batteries." He felt a smile crease his face. "Sometimes they really indulged us, allowing us to camp out for a couple of days. My dad even built a firepit, but we could only use it when he was there to keep an eye on us. We roasted marshmallows and hot dogs and felt so freaking special. Many times, neighborhood kids joined us."

"That sounds really delightful."

His smile widened a shade. "I'll never forget the smell of the smoke that somehow always came my way. Or the racket of the crickets chirping when it grew quiet. The sound of frogs in nearby water. Catching minnows with a net, then setting them free. Pollywogs fascinated us when they started to grow their frog legs. An amazing transformation even after we knew why it was happening."

"It does sound wonderful," she murmured, enjoying the way all the hard edges seemed to leave his face as he remembered.

"Maybe the memories have been enhanced by time. I don't care. I'll keep them the way they are now."

"I'll second that."

He regarded her as he finished his Danish. She'd barely picked at hers. He was sure, despite her denial, that hearing him stirring had dragged her out of sleep. He'd worried her by telling her he might be a target.

He'd noticed how she'd checked all the windows and doors and closed all the curtains.

He asked, "What are you worried about? Me telling you that I might be a target?"

Her attention snapped to him. "I'm not sure I believe that."

"Neither am I."

"Okay." She stared down at her plate, at her barely touched pastry. "Belief is a dangerous thing sometimes. Best not to ignore the possibility, though."

He agreed, but he didn't want to press the issue. She had enough to concern her without worrying about him. He sought to give her a bit of reassurance. "I'm a hard guy to kill."

"That's patently obvious. You're sitting across from me and, given your job, being here is an achievement."

"It shouldn't be, but I guess it is." Unable to stop himself, he reached across the table to take her hand. His heart stuttered when her fingers wrapped around his and tightened.

There was such fatigue and sorrow on her face. He felt bad for bringing all this to her door. His brother's murder clearly concerned her, and she would have worked as long and hard as it took to solve it even without him. But he'd added to her concerns.

He spoke. "I'm sorry I've made this case harder on you."

She made a slight negative movement with her head. "It would have been hard anyway."

"But the sheriff was keeping you out of it until I arrived."

Her eyes grew fierce. "I *wanted* to be on this case. It wouldn't have been long before I'd have demanded it. Yeah, I knew Larry, but I didn't know him well enough to lose my objectivity. Don't blame yourself for that."

His brow creased as anger with himself began to grow. "Then I showed up, looking like trouble. You had to run around to try to prevent me from going ballistic all over the county."

At that, a small laugh escaped her. "It hasn't been that difficult."

"Because you were willing to work with me. But I'll be honest. Much as I hate to admit it, when I arrived here I did want to tear a few people apart. Obviously, I didn't know who."

She raised a brow. "Do you still want to?"

"Tear someone apart? Sometimes, but the urge isn't as strong as when I arrived here. I think you'd be safe not worrying about that."

She squeezed his hand again, then withdrew hers. He regretted the absence of her touch immediately. Damn, he was starting to get tangled up between grief, anger and the pull he felt toward Cat.

She nibbled some more at her Danish, then brought the coffeepot to the table, refilling both their mugs. "We might have made some real strides today," she remarked.

"Possibly. There's always some uncertainty in a combat situation. I'm used to it. But this feels like nothing *except* uncertainty."

"That's where it's at right now," she agreed. "Sometimes murders never get solved. I won't lie to you. But something different was going on with Larry. I'm convinced he was a target, not an accident."

He agreed. "Why hasn't his house been released? There has to be a reason."

He watched her chew her lower lip. Then she said, "The murder was brutal. We're preventing curiosity seekers from sneaking in there as long as we can."

That probably told him more than he wanted to know. He yanked himself away from images that immediately popped to mind. If anyone knew brutal, he did. Her choice of modifier certainly spoke volumes. Given what she did for a living, she'd probably seen multiple murder scenes.

He felt sick, facing a suspicion he'd avoided but now couldn't. What the hell had been done to Larry, and how much did he really want to know?

But Cat's consideration of the possibility that someone had tracked Larry from elsewhere also spoke volumes to him. She felt something much bigger than a burglary had occurred.

But she wouldn't talk in detail without evidence. She'd made that clear at the outset, and he had to respect her position. She might speculate about motives, but that kind of spitballing was part of her job. Turning things around and around until she saw her way to a solution.

"Let's go for a walk," she said.

He wasn't opposed, but he studied her. "Am I giving you cabin fever?"

"Right now this job is giving me cabin fever. The research must be done."

"But at the office, you'd have a lot more people to talk to than just me."

"That's true, but I'd still spend almost all the time reading. Plus, this new idea…well, I want to talk it over with Gage, if you don't mind."

"Sure."

Ten minutes later they stepped outside into the night wearing jackets. The temperatures were falling again, and Duke wondered if he smelled snow on the air.

It was easy, though, to bend into the night breeze, strolling alongside Cat.

He didn't need another run. What he needed was company.

Two MEN, DRESSED completely in black, with ski masks over their faces and black camouflage cream around their eyes, came around the rear of Matt Keller's tiny little house. Concealed by the night and their clothing, they looked like darker shadows in the pale starlight. The moon was gone, concealing them even more.

They had scoped the house a couple of hours earlier after darkness had arrived, peeking into windows until they had a mental image of the interior. Mostly they knew which room they needed to get to.

Unfortunately, that room was a tiny ell, barely a jog in the hallway beside the bathroom and just in front of Matt's bedroom. Behind the ell, however, was a mud porch that might be useful. But they agreed they'd prefer their entry point to be as far as possible from the bedroom, which meant the front of the house, in case they made any noise while getting past the door.

They were prepared for creaking floors in such an old house. They had night-vision goggles to keep them from stumbling into things. They figured there wouldn't be any hidden obstacles on the floor, because this was a single guy—no dogs, no kids to spread toys around.

They didn't talk; they didn't need to. From here out hand signals would suffice.

They were also prepared to deal with Matt should he discover them. Not the way they had dealt with Larry Duke, but differently, so there'd be no resemblance.

Because spring was just beginning, despite the calendar, most plants offered little concealment. Aiding them, however, Keller had some evergreen shrubs along the front, back and sides of his house. They'd tested them earlier and found they weren't brittle.

The bushes provided a perfect hiding spot as they crouched down in the back, waiting for the entire world to go to sleep.

Except for one damn cop car that drove by every so often. A lot of protection in such a sleepy town. That cop also changed their plan. After a few hours, they realized he was random in his appearances. Back door it would be.

They waited, shifting position just often enough to keep from getting stiff.

Around two thirty, they began to move stealthily, freezing often in case some random person happened to glance out into the night and see some moving shadows. It made for a slower trip from the side of the house to the back door.

Several windows on nearby houses looked straight

into Keller's yard, but the first man figured those windows didn't create as much of a threat as a sharp-eyed cop who was probably hoping for any kind of distraction, even investigating shadows.

The back door proved to be an easy open. A lousy screen-door type of lock, easily broken with little noise.

The floors creaked more than anticipated, slowing them down as they paused frequently to let the noise slip away. No other sounds disturbed the house.

At last they opened the interior door, which let into the hallway. It seemed odd to the first man that the mudroom didn't open to the kitchen, but it didn't really matter. It was close to the office in the ell.

Another few steps and they were inside their target room, through a door that had been left open. Searching everything took a while, too, because they were looking for tiny stuff, like a disc or flash drive, and even into files in a cabinet, hoping to spy a label that might come from a different source. And they were trying to be silent.

They found a bunch of those flash drives and were getting ready to leave with the laptop computer when a voice startled them.

"What the hell?"

They'd been ready for this. Man Three grabbed Matt Keller from behind, wrapping one arm around his chest and clamping a gloved hand over his mouth.

Man One stepped in to finish it.

As they walked, Cat was surprised to feel Duke touch her arm. She looked at him and saw him make the sign with two fingers to his eyes, then point toward one house.

Matt Keller's house. *Oh damn.* She peered into the night, trying to see what had alerted Duke. Then she noticed a couple of shadows that appeared out of place. Wrong size for a tree and shaped all wrong.

They weren't moving, however, so she was ready to dismiss them as a trick of light. But then she saw movement, and it wasn't the movement of a tree or large bush swaying.

Two people? Crouched down? She hadn't worn her gun, but now she wished she had.

She glanced at the house and thought she saw a light inside. Matt. Without hesitation, she ran toward the front door.

"Want me to chase them?" Duke's voice drew her up short.

He was off before she could say a word, although at that point she had a bigger concern: Matt Keller.

Without any more discussion, Duke took off into the night toward the alley.

Cat's attention centered fully on Matt. If someone had broken into Matt's house, was he still alive? Or had he been tortured like Larry Duke?

She couldn't waste time wondering about the perps until she made sure Matt was reasonably okay.

The front door was locked. She sped around to the back, running because Matt's life might depend on speed. They'd had to break in somehow, and a back door was concealed from the street.

Assuming those guys had gotten in at all.

Inside, she moved with reasonable caution while her heart hammered, aware that someone might be there other than Matt. After she'd checked the front rooms, she looked down the hallway. There was only one closed door, and light spilled from a little ell.

She checked that and the bathroom as quickly as she could, barely noting the mess in the ell, then called out, "Matt? Matt?"

No sound answered her. Cat's heart nearly stopped. *Oh my God.*

"Matt? Are you here?"

She thought she heard something from behind the closed door. Muffled. She couldn't wait any longer. She turned the knob and opened the door, prepared for just about anything.

When she flipped the light switch just inside, she found Matt lying on his bed, ankles and wrists wrapped in zip ties. His arms were above his head, his cuffed wrists tied to the headboard by rope. Duct tape covered his mouth.

Without another moment's hesitation, she hurried over to rip the tape from his mouth. "Are you hurt?"

"Mostly bruised, I think." His voice shook. "It was like being tackled by two linebackers. Damn, what happened?"

"I think you might have been robbed. And since I don't have my radio on me, can I use your phone?"

"Yes. Then get these damn ties off me. They're too tight."

She grabbed the phone beside the bed and called the emergency number.

Then she went on a hunt to find a tool to cut those ties. She already heard the sirens.

DUKE RETURNED TO a swirl of cops and EMTs. Matt Keller was being carried out on a gurney over his protests that he was just a little bruised. Some injuries might not be immediately apparent, one of the EMTs told Keller. Better safe than sorry.

Immense relief filled him, knowing that Matt was still able to argue.

He could tell that, inside, Cat had taken charge of the scene. He heard her telling two cops to tape off the ell. From what little he could see from the front, it looked as if a tornado had come through, but it was obvious even to his eyes that a computer had been stolen. And what else?

They'd probably have to wait on Matt's return to find out.

He stayed out of the way by the front door after his one attempt to get inside, hardly surprised when a cop informed him of the dangers in contaminating a crime scene.

Another twenty minutes passed until Cat was satisfied and had explained to at least two cops what she had found upon her entry. So the guy had been tackled, tied and gagged.

For Duke it was like a cherry on the cake. It confirmed his worst suspicions. What he'd seen—or failed to see—when he chased those men had been the first confirmation. He needed to tell Cat.

When she joined him, she said, "Let them work. We'll go to the sidewalk."

He nodded and followed. He figured she'd hardly notice the cold now. With doors open, the house was probably reaching the outside temperature, the change negligible.

"Did you get any identifying information?" she said the minute they reached the sidewalk.

"Not exactly. Tell me how Matt was bound."

She gave him an impatient look, probably resenting the way he tossed the question back to her instead of just telling her. She sketched what she had found. "Now you."

He nodded. "This was professional."

He watched her face stiffen, an instant of resistance followed by huge dismay. "Seriously? How can you know that?"

"By the way they melted into the night. No kids did this. It was someone who knew how to handle an op like this, how to get away."

"But why?" Then she paused. "Of course. We've been talking about it." She cussed, a word he'd never before heard her use. He felt the same way.

"Tomorrow," he told her, "we need to go see Ben, warn him."

"But Larry was keeping that relationship a secret!"

"He probably was, but that doesn't mean no one knows about it. Secrets have a way of getting out somehow."

She lowered her head. "Damn it, Duke."

"Yeah."

Cat visibly shook herself. "You might as well go home. Nothing you can do here. I'll follow as soon as I can."

He nodded, then walked off into the night.

Chapter Ten

When the sun rose in the morning, the three men sat in a different gully, one chosen because it was even more concealed, this one surrounded by whispering pines, buried in shadows. Yesterday had involved too much exposure around town for them not to be concerned.

The night's chill had lingered, possibly grown deeper, and the clouds overhead didn't help any.

"Yesterday was a screwup," said the second man. He'd drunk four cups of coffee already, and the two laptops sat beside him on rocks.

The first man's response was an indirect rebuke. "You get anywhere with Duke's computer?"

"Actually, I might have. I need to look a little more. But these batteries only last ten to twelve hours. I'm gonna need more juice before long."

"The other computer?"

"I haven't had it long enough," the second man replied sourly. "Hell, you just brought it in."

The third man agreed. "There's still no point getting in a fight. We're all nervous. Uneasy."

Man Two persisted. "I think we got a problem. *He*,"

he said, pointing at the first man, "went into public yesterday. Doesn't matter it was a truck stop. Someone still could have noticed him."

Man One shook his head. "The only time I opened my mouth was to order. Amazing what you can learn simply by *listening*."

"Then there's last night. You nearly got caught during that stupid, stupid burglary. You even got chased from the scene."

"We *weren't* caught," Man Three argued defensively.

"I bet someone had an idea that you two were something more than juveniles."

"Who was that guy who chased us?" Man Three asked. "Do you have any idea?"

The first man remained silent, but the other two could tell he had a suspicion. Why didn't he tell them?

For a brief spell, it appeared that the second man was about to erupt. Unusual sounds emerged from the back of his throat. Finally he said, "I bet you didn't find anything, either."

Man One spoke sarcastically. "We won't know that until you look at those flash drives."

"I need some time. Larry Duke's laptop is getting low on power. That'll leave me with just the new one. Hell, I was on Larry's most of the night."

"You said you might have found something."

"Maybe. I need to look a little more, but there's this guy who turns up in some old emails. Repeatedly. And he seems to live out here. Ben Williams."

Man One leaned forward, his eyes still bruised by the long night. "How do you know he's around here?"

"I ran a search."

CAT DIDN'T GO home until after nine in the morning. She'd not only had to make sure the investigation teams were doing everything they needed to, but she had to fill out a report, detailing her entire involvement, from when she saw the two figures running away to finding Matt tied in his bed.

After that, she caught up with Gage and informed him about her and Duke's theory.

Gage sat forward so suddenly that she heard his chair thud. He must have been tipped backward far enough to lift some of the wheels off the floor. Dangerous, but she didn't think Gage was a man who worried about danger. If he had been, he'd never have gone undercover for the DEA.

"Someone from Duke's past?" he asked. "Not Larry's but his?"

"Both, actually. We'd begun to arrive there partly because of Larry's horrific murder—and by the way, I didn't give him details, but I probably said enough—and the fallout from Larry's investigation that involved the Army. Duke thinks someone who is still in danger from that investigation might be worried about whether Larry was writing a book about it."

"Was he?"

"I don't know, Gage. The man was a clam about his work. If his editor knew anything about what he was working on, she didn't say. And since he wasn't on the paper's time, she probably didn't know. Larry never shared anything until he put it in print."

"Great help." Gage leaned back, rubbing his chin. "What else?"

"Duke said the guys who ran away from Matt Keller's

house last night were trained. Not some kids, but people who knew how to be covert. He went after them, but they slipped away like ghosts."

Gage's eyes narrowed. "I'd go with Duke's opinion on that. He's got enough experience to know. Hell."

"There's still nothing linking the burglaries," Cat pointed out scrupulously.

"There wouldn't be if they know what they're doing. Inexperienced juveniles might not be smart enough to conceal it. Why didn't Larry get tied up, too? And why was Matt tied up but not killed? Serious questions here."

"When was the last time there was a string of burglaries around here?"

Gage shook his head, then gave a mirthless half smile. "We've had a few. Kids. I remember one when they gave themselves up by their choices in clothing." His humorless smile turned back into a frown. "I don't like this."

"Me neither. And to frost the cake, Duke is wondering if he might be a target, too."

"Oh, for the love of— Why?"

"Because a person or several persons in the Army might think Duke was a source for his brother. Even though he wasn't and didn't know about the murder-for-hire thing until it broke in the paper. From what Duke has said, his career has gone by the wayside."

Gage just shook his head. This was a lot to take in, she thought, watching him absorb it. "Which story was this again?"

Cat started. "Oh man, I didn't tell you. Larry did an exposé about two years ago that uncovered three soldiers involved in a murder-for-hire operation. Duke thinks some officers had to have been involved some way. He could explain his thinking to you better than I can." She spread her hands. "I don't know the Army the way he does."

"Few of us do," Gage said absently. Then he snapped back again. "This settles better in my gut than our original random theories about Larry's murder. What are you planning to do next?"

"It's okay for me to get involved again?"

"You already are, from what I can tell. Do you see me objecting?"

Despite the night she'd just had, Cat had to smile. "I haven't heard it."

"And if you had, you'd become conveniently deaf. Sort of like the cat you're named after."

He leaned forward again and reached for a pencil, drumming it on his desk. "What's your next move?"

"Duke wants to go see Ben Williams. To warn him what might be happening. Is that okay?"

"At this point, I'm saying yes. Your case, your decision."

Cat walked out of there feeling a whole lot better. Well, in a few ways. The major part of this was going to be impossible to feel any better about.

WHEN SHE GOT HOME, Duke was waiting for her with coffee and a bag of buttery croissants. The man definitely knew how to spoil a woman.

Feeling almost as if the kitchen table had become the center of her life, she joined him, holding her mug in both hands, trying to warm up her fingers. He had placed a croissant on a plate in front of her, and the open butter dish with a knife.

"Aren't you going to eat?" she asked.

"I already did. I might have more later. How did it go?"

"It went."

"Any news about Matt Keller?"

She shook her head. "Not really. They're holding him for observation for a few hours, but no reports of serious damage. Apparently some good bruises, though. We'll have to go with him tomorrow for an inventory to find out what's missing, if anything."

"Did someone talk to him?"

"A deputy went to the hospital to interview him. Right now, I don't know any more." She raised weary eyes to look at him. "I don't think I'd want to go home today if I were Matt."

Duke sighed. "I wouldn't, either."

Cat felt a stab of anger. "No, but you'll waltz around this county acting like you don't believe you might be a target."

His expression grew flat. He spoke levelly. "I can leave if you're worried."

"Worried about what? Your safety? Of course I am. Worried about myself—no way!"

He frowned. "I'm the last person you should worry about. Anything these perps know, I know a thousand times better. Trust me, I may be infantry now, but I used to be Airborne. A long-range sniper rifle is the only thing I need to worry about, and snipers are few and far between."

She liked his confidence but wasn't as sure herself.

"I've got to get to bed," she announced. "I won't be good for anything without some sleep. I'll phone Ben when I get up."

But before she rose, she gave him another bit of information. "I'm in charge of these investigations now."

Then she marched off to bed, hoping her pillow would silence her racing thoughts and give her a break from all of this.

It had been bad enough when she found Larry. The weeds, though, seemed to just keep getting deeper. She needed some fuel for her tank.

"ANYTHING YET?" THE first man asked the second.

The second guy tossed another flash drive on the small but growing pile beside him. "No. Nothing seems to be hidden or locked. But this guy might have some trouble with the IRS."

"Why?" asked the third man.

"Because we may have all his business files and spreadsheets. He owns a store, and the litany of numbers is mind-numbing. I'm guessing he kept the information on both his laptop and backup flash drives, which he wouldn't need if he was using the cloud for storage."

The first man merely nodded, but the third snorted in disgust. "Cripes," Man Three said. "What the hell are we doing out here?"

"My guess," said the first man, "would be any information related in any way to the Army. So nothing personal? Nothing encrypted? Nothing out of place?"

"I'm not done yet. As for personal, I have his 1040-As for the last five years."

"That'd be great if he was a political candidate," offered the third guy. But he still sounded disgusted.

"If you don't find anything there," the first man said, "the three of us will scope out Ben Williams's place. He might be a better possibility because he's known Larry Duke for…how long?"

Man Two looked up. "Emails stretch back almost four years."

"Four years. Of all the people around here, he might have had Larry Duke's trust. Better than those poker buddies we've been trying to track down."

The two others nodded. "Then what?" asked Man Three.

"We plan. We might be able to go in tonight."

The second man looked between the other two. "What the hell happened last night?"

"Somebody chased us while we were leaving Keller's place."

"Daniel Duke," said the first man.

"Then you know him?" asked Man Two.

"Only ran into him once."

"So he won't recognize you."

"No reason he should. But if he gets in my way again, I'm going to take him out." The first man held out his hands and squeezed them into fists repeatedly.

"But you said…" The second guy trailed off. Then he changed course. "If we don't find anything at this Williams guy's house, what then?"

"Then I'm calling the jerk who sent us out here, and

I'm telling him we quit. I've had enough of this, and I'm sick of the three of us being exposed on a mission that's poorly directed and conceived."

For once, nobody mentioned the money.

Then some snowflakes began to fall. Another complication.

CAT WOKE FROM some unexpectedly steamy dreams about Duke. *Oh man*, she thought as she scrubbed her eyes awake. She had believed she'd managed to put all that away in some locked box in her brain. It was a complication neither of them needed—not that he'd be in any kind of mood for it, considering why he'd come out here.

She shouldn't be in the mood for it, either, but it seemed she was. The man had leaped past too many of her defenses in such a short time. When she thought of him now, she no longer felt the spark of irritation. Instead it was as if a kitten had curled up with her.

Dang, he was no kitten. A lion for sure.

She forced her feelings back into the mental safe, then remembered a couple of times when she had thought Duke's gaze reflected desire. She must have been mistaken. He couldn't possibly want *her*, and not under these circumstances.

She indulged a few minutes remembering how broad his shoulders were, how narrow his hips were. The way he smelled after a run and a shower. His comfortable lope when he ran, and his equally comfortable walking stride.

Quite the figure of a man. But more than that, she'd

watched him deal with horrific things, watched him face emotions that must have him knotted inside. She was impressed.

She showered and donned some civvies, her favorite jeans and a sweatshirt against the cold that seemed to fill the house.

She paused at the thermostat and turned the heat up a couple of degrees. Reassuringly, the furnace started.

She'd half expected to find Duke in the kitchen, and there he was, phone pressed to his ear, a mug of coffee in front of him, along with some croissants.

At least she didn't have to think about food yet. She grabbed a croissant for herself, along with a mug of coffee, and sat down with him. She buttered her pastry while he talked.

"I'm just wondering if there's any scuttlebutt about who is pushing back at me. I know my CO is involved in some way because he signs the reports, but there's got to be someone higher, and I can't ask Jeffries. He'd deny it."

He paused then said, "Thanks, Crash. Whatever's in the wind."

"Crash?" Cat asked as Duke put down his phone.

"Nickname. He and I became buddies back at the academy. Good man."

"You trust him not to tell anyone you're asking?"

"Absolutely. I phoned a handful of others I feel the same way about. Maybe we'll get some intel. I don't expect it right away, though."

"Nope," she agreed and bit into her croissant. She was glad he had people he could trust with this. One of the things she liked about living here was that the people she spent the most time with were people who seemed totally trustworthy. Duke's friends probably went back a lot further.

"Is there some kind of code?" she asked.

"I'm getting skewered on it right now. The code not to talk. But that's no guarantee that lips are always zipped. Obviously. And things can be said within the Army that should never be shared with nonsoldiers."

She'd pretty much gathered that from an earlier conversation, but she felt edgy now that he'd made the calls. Word might get back to the wrong ears.

Nothing she could say or do now, however. Not that she could have argued him out of the calls. He probably would have turned into a brick wall again. "So you think your CO is involved?"

He shrugged. "It's possible. He is, after all, writing my performance reports. On the other hand, he may be getting some pressure and not even know why. He's got a career to consider, too."

That sounded ugly. She tried to shift to something less disturbing. They already had plenty of reasons to be disturbed. "Did you sleep?"

"I snagged a few z's."

Her landline rang, and she went to answer it. A short time later, her stomach plummeted to the ground. She hung up and faced Duke, braced for his reaction. Her mouth turned so dry she wasn't sure she could speak. "Larry's body is on the way back."

His entire face tightened. "Good." The word came out sharply, edged in darkness.

"They'll take him to the funeral home, the only one here. Do you want him shipped back with you?"

It took him a few minutes as he seemed to stare into some bleak place inside him. "I think Ben should decide."

She did, too.

He raised his head, suddenly looking gaunt. "Cat… Cat…"

Not knowing what else to do, she moved to wrap her arms around him from behind. Her heart was breaking for him, yet she still enjoyed his scent, the hard strength of his shoulders.

Damn, she was losing it. So inappropriate right now.

But he surprised her, reaching around and tugging her until she could sit on his lap.

"Cat," he whispered roughly, "this doesn't make sense, but I…"

She got it. Totally. She didn't care if it didn't make sense, didn't care if this didn't fit with the concerns that swirled around them. She felt it, too. Needed it.

His arms snaked around her, tightening until he held her close to his heat, until her face rested between his shoulder and neck. She closed her eyes, reveling in his hug, and rested her hand on his chest. The man was nearly as hard as rock, and his embrace made her feel so soft…

Then she felt a shudder rip through him. Oh God, it was hitting him—hitting him hard. Whatever form of denial he'd been using had just been torn away by the news that Larry's body would arrive soon.

Another shudder took him, but when she tried to

move, he just held her closer. She didn't want to get away; she wanted to be in a better position to comfort him.

But maybe this was what he needed? She couldn't decide that for him. So she relaxed and remained silent while grief gripped him. Aching for him and feeling utterly foolish for thinking this might ever have been anything else.

She was sure he'd lost others in his life, given the nature of his career, but this had to be different, even worse. As close as he must become with his fellow soldiers in unimaginable circumstances, there must be an even deeper connection with the brother you'd grown up with. Families of different kinds.

As carefully as he held her, as much as his arms supported her, she began to feel restless. This wasn't exactly a natural position, not for long.

His shuddering had passed, and maybe this was a time she could move. His arms hadn't loosened any, and she didn't want to make him feel any worse, but still...

Carefully, slowly, she pulled away a little.

"I'm sorry," he said, his voice low and quiet. "You've got to be uncomfortable."

"A little," she admitted, "but don't apologize."

Slipping off his lap, she bent a little side to side while keeping her attention on him. His eyes were closed, but there was no sign of tears on his cheeks. He'd gone through the storm without a tear. She'd have been blubbering her head off, as she knew from when her mother had died. Tears were a release, an expression of feelings for which there were no adequate words.

"Duke?" She spoke quietly.

His eyes opened, and he looked hollow. "Yeah?"

"Can I get you something? Coffee? Beer? Milk?" Useless questions, answering only her own need to do something for him. "Do you want anything?"

"You," he said.

Her heart slammed, and her knees turned to water.

CAT BARELY REMEMBERED getting to the bedroom. Like a scene from a movie, the world turned into a blur as they pulled clothes away and stumbled into her bedroom, kissing wildly all the while. She'd never believed those scenes. Now she did, with the haziest of memories to support it.

All that mattered was how quickly they'd come to be lying naked on her bed. The curtains were still drawn, and little light seeped into the room, leaving a twilight that felt right for the unreality that had seized her. Bright light would have interfered, made everything stand out starkly. Would have kept her from slipping away into a place where nothing existed except Duke and the desire that poured through her like lava.

Heavy breathing. Palms stroking skin as if trying to create fire from friction and unleashing a very different kind of fire. Damn, his skin felt good, and his touch felt even better. She skimmed over what felt like scars, stories yet to be told.

She gasped as he caressed her, a merciless reconnaissance of her every curve and hollow. His hands and fingers took liberties that left her moaning as he teased her breasts, then slipped his hand between her legs, pressing until she arched, needing ever so much more. She grabbed his shoulders like a life preserver in dangerous waters, feeling as if she would drown in him and never return.

Then his mouth followed his hands. She nearly went mad, writhing under his every touch, trying to reach him and reciprocate, but he wouldn't let her. He was in command this time, and she finally let it be. His need for control was hardly surprising, and she was willing to grant it to him. Another time...

Coherent thoughts were few and far between and becoming rarer by the second. Swept away by his demanding desire, she let him carry her to wherever he wanted.

Like the eternal current carrying them both. She felt herself rising as if on a rogue wave, higher and higher until she felt a fear of tipping into the trough below. Then a fear of not tipping over at all.

He slipped inside her, filling her until she ached from it. When he started moving, she followed helplessly, needing it, needing him.

She fell over the edge, feeling him fall with her, jerking suddenly against her, giving her one last trip to the top before she tumbled into peace.

THEY LAY TOGETHER in a tangled mess of bodies and bedcovers. At some point Duke rose up to grab a pillow and place it under both their heads, but then she disappeared once again into his embrace.

Cat had never had such an experience. Never. Delicious, fraught with a maelstrom of sensation and feelings that kept her on a scary edge until the moment when release set her free.

Wild.

Never before had she felt quite as satisfied, either. As if no part of her had escaped the experience.

He stirred a little, his hand running along her back. "Magic," he murmured.

"Yeah," she breathed. Oh yeah.

Then, bringing the beautiful moments to an abrupt end, he stiffened. "Ben."

"Oh God." She wiggled, breaking free, and sat up. "You're sure he might be in danger?"

"I don't want to risk it."

"Neither do I. You grab a shower while I call him. We'll go over there, if you want."

"I want. But…"

Cat paused as she pulled on her robe over her cooling body. "What?"

"This isn't romantic."

She leaned over him, resting her hands on the bed. "If the past hour wasn't romantic, I don't know what is. I'm a grown-up, Duke. I don't need flowers, or lingering in bed, or taking showers together. Another time. Now get your butt in gear."

"Yes, ma'am."

She thought she heard a tremor of amusement in his voice as she hurried to the phone.

Before she could pick it up, it began ringing. Her heart slammed with the fear. What now? She had a sudden memory of the old sheriff, Nate Tate, remarking once on another case since she'd moved here, "This county's going to hell in a handbasket." Apparently, it had been his signature complaint, but never in her time here had it seemed more true.

"Jansen," she said into the phone.

"Gage," said the familiar voice. "I got the forensics report."

She swallowed hard, sensing what was coming. "It's bad."

"As bad as our worst fears. You don't need the details, but Larry was definitely tortured. Maybe for an hour."

"Oh my God," she whispered, closing her eyes. "I suspected, but…"

"We all did. Being human, we hoped it wasn't true. Larry's remains should be arriving at the funeral home tomorrow afternoon. Unless there's another plan."

"Duke wants to talk it over with Ben first. I think we're going out to see him tonight."

Gage sighed. "Damn it. I never wanted to see anything like this ever again. We've got to find this bastard so I can nail his hide to a wall. And Duke gets to use the nail gun first."

"I think he's going to want a hammer."

CAT WAS SHAKING so hard that she sat at the table before calling Ben. A whole bucket of horror was about to drop into the laps of these two men, Ben and Duke, and she wished she didn't have to be part of informing them.

She glanced at the phone in her hand. She had to call Ben and try to do it without giving him reason to guess that the case had just leapfrogged past gruesome to horrific. She drew a few steadying breaths, centering herself in professional reactions, then made the call.

"Hey, Ben. Duke and I want to come to see you. Okay by you?"

"Absolutely. I took some time off, and sitting out here by myself is driving me nuts. Too much empty space to fill with sorrow and anger."

"I hear you. Duke will share that, I think."

"I'm sure. That's part of the reason it'll be good to see him. Plus, way back when, we were acquainted."

But Duke had been too busy trying to avoid his own grief by chasing a killer to be thinking about Ben. "Thanks," she said. "Want us to pick up some dinner?"

"If you go by Maude's, a steak sandwich is always welcome."

"Done."

WHILE DUKE WENT to Maude's to pick up dinner, Cat visited the sheriff's office. "I'm taking two shotguns and a rifle, and some body armor," she said to Sarah Ironheart, who was sitting at the duty desk.

Gage must have the hearing of a cat, she thought, as his head poked out his door. "Cat?"

"Coming."

She hurried back, aware that heads were pivoting to look at her. She was past caring that she'd caused the room to seethe with curiosity. She couldn't just take the guns without checking them out.

"You expecting trouble?" Gage asked, motioning her to close the door.

"Maybe. I don't know. Duke is worried that Ben

could be a target in this mess, too. If this guy is looking for information of some kind, eventually he'd light
on Ben, wouldn't he?"

Gage rubbed his chin and nodded. "Maybe so. You
want some backup?"

"For what? A feeling? No. I want to make sure we're
armed. Just in case. That's all. The same as going out
on patrol or answering a call. Because you never know."

"All right." He paused. "About this report…"

"The forensics?" she interrupted. "I don't want to
hear any more today. Maybe tomorrow. Right now I've
got to be with two grieving men, and the less I know,
the better."

"Can't argue with that. Take the guns. Goggles, too,
if you want. And plenty of ammo. Hell, just take one of
the patrol vehicles."

She thought about that. "Advertising."

He just shook his head. "Do it your way, Cat. Your
case, your decision."

The guns would fit well enough in the back of Duke's
truck under the tonneau. Two Mossberg riot guns and
a long rifle. Boxes of ammo. Clips. Three sets of night-
vision goggles. Three sets of chest armor. Ready for war.

Part of her wanted to find this ridiculous, but the rest
of her just couldn't do it. Larry's murderer was still out
there, a man who would torture someone for an hour or
more. Two men, she corrected herself. Duke had seen
two men running from Matt's house.

No, she wanted Ben protected even if she had to demand he come stay with her along with Duke. And if

Duke decided he needed to stay with Ben, then the two of them were sure as hell going to be adequately armed.

But taking a patrol vehicle? No. Why draw attention? What if someone had Ben's house under observation? Sure, tell 'em a cop was inside.

And Duke was right. Larry and Ben might have tried to keep their relationship on the q.t., but people still found things out. Still made connections and assumptions. Then there was the fact that Larry had shared it with her. He had just dropped it, asking her to keep it to herself. What if he'd told someone else and they'd shared it further?

God, Duke was right. Too many maybes.

Hope for the best, prepare for the worst.

SHORTLY SHE AND Duke were driving along county roads toward Ben's house. Bags from Maude's were tucked behind the seats. The back end was loaded, literally and figuratively.

As they started to reach quiet roads, snow began to fall, thicker than the few flakes that had fluttered down earlier.

"Great," she said. "Weren't there enough complications already?"

He glanced her way as he drove. "You're loaded for bear."

"Believe it. *Fed up* would be a good description. I want this case solved. I always do, but this is one that's eating me alive."

He didn't answer.

What could he say? she wondered. He didn't know

what Gage had told her, which was more than enough to light her fuse. He might suspect, but he didn't know, and she wanted to keep it that way. For now, at least. She couldn't just drop this on Ben, either.

He spoke. "So is Cat short for something?"

She shook her head and glanced at him. "Nope. Just Cat. I asked my mom about it once, and she couldn't explain it except that it had caught her fancy."

"Dad?"

"He never had any input. Gone before I was born. Anyway, once I got past the teasing, I decided I like it."

"You should. It's unique. Like you."

Here she was talking about her name. She kept giving herself mental kicks, trying to calm down. She shouldn't have let the news put her into hyperdrive. But, like Gage had said, they were human and had hoped they were wrong, but she'd known. They'd known. Maybe they just hadn't wanted to accept it.

"Listen," he said after another mile or so, "about earlier…"

"You don't have to say anything," she interjected swiftly. An apology right now would kill her. There was still a glow to be had from their sex, and she wanted to hang on to it. Tightly.

"I *do* have to say something. You weren't just a distraction. Not an escape. I wanted you. I've been wanting you ever since you confronted me in front of the department store."

She snorted quietly. "So you like women who stand up to you?"

"I sure don't like doormats. I don't wilt."

"I noticed."

It was his turn to yield a short laugh. "Seriously, Cat, it was wonderful, and I hope we can do it again when all kinds of ugly things aren't whipping around us. When we can just take our time and savor it."

She liked the sound of that. She turned a little in her seat. "I'd like that, too."

"I just wanted you to know I wasn't using you. Every other time I wanted to have sex with you, I've stopped myself because I couldn't say that with certainty. Now I can."

She had to admit to herself that it felt better to know that. She'd told herself it didn't matter, but it seemed it did.

"Still," she couldn't prevent herself from saying, "there's no real future in it." That was one she had to face squarely.

"Future?" He shook his head. "Lady, you're talking to a soldier. Long-distance relationships aren't an obstacle. Just saying."

She hadn't thought about that before, either. *Hmm.*

But as they drew closer to Ben's house, she felt her stomach trying to knot. There was danger ahead, although she didn't know of what kind. Emotional explosions? Ben having a breakdown? Like she could blame him if he did.

When they pulled up beside Ben's house, he came out to greet them. Before he and Duke could do more than shake hands, Cat opened the tailgate, ready to pass out the armament.

"Don't say I don't come prepared. I've got two riot

guns, a rifle and a heavy bag of ammo. Oh, and night-vision goggles and armor. Who's carrying what?"

Cat saw Ben stiffen. "What the hell?" he asked.

Duke spoke first. "Let's get this gear inside. Then we'll talk. C'mon."

Ben didn't argue, maybe because he heard an order as an order. Something to be said in favor of military experience, Cat thought sourly as she grabbed the two cases holding the riot guns. Ben took the rifle and the heavy ammo carrier.

"I'll get the food and armor," Duke said. With a gesture, he motioned Ben toward the door. "Step lively, soldier."

That drew a half smile from Ben, who otherwise looked as if he'd been walking through the hallways of hell.

Cat followed Ben inside, hearing the sounds as Duke slammed the tailgate closed, then got the bags of food from the cab. She'd barely had time to lean the riot guns against the wall in a corner before Duke joined them, his hands full, his shoulders burdened by the heavy body armor.

Cold had entered the house through the open door, and it took several minutes before the air heated up again. Nobody shed a jacket while they put Maude's bags in the kitchen.

Then Duke sat down to unzip carrying cases and examine the guns. "Good selection," he said to Cat as she sat across from him on a flowery upright chair. Ben took another chair nearby.

Ben cleared his throat. "Guns?"

Duke didn't exactly answer. "I'd prefer the rifle my-self, if you two are okay with the shotguns."

"I'm okay with anything that can cause trouble to anyone on the other end," Cat said. "Ben?"

"Shotgun is fine with me, too." He cleared his throat. "Why?"

Cat indicated Duke with an open hand. Let him ex-plain this maze. She wasn't at all sure they weren't over-reacting, and this might not be a good time to inject any doubt.

"First things," Duke said. "Larry will be back in town tomorrow."

Ben leaned forward, resting his elbows on his knees, burying his face in his hands. "Oh God," he whispered.

The pain in this room was palpable. Two men deal-ing with heart-crushing grief for which there'd never be a cure. Cat felt tears well in her own eyes and blinked them back.

A few minutes passed. Then Ben lifted his head. His face was marked by two tear streaks running from his eyes. "They didn't let me know. Of course not. I don't matter. It's not like we were married."

Duke spoke, his voice gruff. "You matter to *me*. And I haven't been officially notified yet, either. Cat got the call as the lead investigator, and she told me. Now we're telling you."

Ben leaned back, closing his eyes. "Yeah," he mur-mured. "It's just…"

Too much, Cat thought. How many avenues were closed to Larry and Ben unless they married? She could only begin to guess at it. A million rights were defined by blood relationships and marital contracts.

Ben spoke again, his tone leaden. "Let me know what you decide about the funeral, Duke. Are you taking him back East?"

Duke cussed and rose. He looked overwhelming in the small space. "Ben, I'm not planning anything without your blessing. I may have the right, but I'm giving you the right to decide everything. I'm not taking him back East unless you want it. If you want him here, he stays here. Got it?"

Ben nodded.

Cat stared up at Duke, admiring him more in that moment than she ever had. He might be tough, even hard as nails at times, but apparently his heart was as big as everything else about him.

Ben took a few more minutes, steadying himself against the pain. Then he stirred. "Okay," he said quietly. "What's up other than dinner from Maude's? As in the arsenal."

"I could have brought more," Cat said, trying a lighter moment. "I wasn't sure how useful pistols would be, but I threw a few in the truck if we want them."

"Pistols." Ben's eyes widened. "Are you expecting an invasion? Where are the flash-bangs? The grenades? The fifty-cal machine gun?"

She was grateful to see him rise to attempted humor. Some things you couldn't just deal with at one time. Ben needed to shake it off for a little while. To give himself an emotional break. Well, this was certainly going to be different.

Duke leaned forward. "We can talk over dinner before it gets too cold, or we can do one or the other first. Up to you."

"I'm curious as hell what the two of you are worried about, but let's eat. I don't remember…" Ben shrugged. "I think I haven't eaten since yesterday."

Cat felt good about being able to slip into gear. "Then let's go, gentlemen."

Ben had a large trestle table in his farm kitchen, and they laid out their food, along with plates, utensils and napkins. Three foam boxes yielded the steak sandwiches, another a large salad, and the final one was dessert: Maude's peach cobbler. A feast.

It amused her a bit, too. She'd never been big on dessert, but Duke seemed to favor it.

Ben broke out some beers, and soon they were seated at one end of the table, Ben at the head, Cat and Duke on either side. They draped jackets over the backs of their chairs.

The crusty sandwich bread was still fresh, not soaked through yet from the steak juices. It smelled so good she could have slipped into a gourmet heaven.

Reality wouldn't allow that.

Duke spoke, answering Ben's questions that seemed to be hanging urgently. "Okay, here's the deal."

Ben nodded, his mouth full.

"We think Larry's murder may be related to that story Larry wrote about the murder-for-hire scheme."

Ben swallowed, then choked a little. He drained some beer to wash the food down, then looked at both of them. "Tell me you're joking." But as soon as the words tumbled out, more of them followed. Ben's face reflected an element of shock. "Damn it, Larry."

Duke responded. "I've been saying a lot of that."

"Damn it," Ben said again. "Damn it, Duke, that was one of the first things I thought of when I learned Larry was murdered. Damn it."

Ben jumped up from the table, paced the length of the kitchen, then disappeared. Cat could hear his footfalls in the next rooms.

She looked at Duke. "He thought of it, too."

Duke nodded. "Nobody wants to, but we both know certain types in uniform. We know the code."

Ben returned with reddened eyes after a couple of minutes and sat down, starting to eat again. Cat followed suit. If this night turned long for some reason, she'd regret failing to eat even though her appetite had died.

Ben had been thinking as he absorbed the news. "I wondered. Then I wondered if any of them thought I might be a source. Like you, Duke. Then, the last day or so, I've been wondering if they might come after me, too. If that's the reason. But that cat was already out of the bag!"

"I would have thought so." Duke finished his sandwich, allowing Ben time to adjust to this.

There was more, Cat knew, but she'd let Duke explain it to Ben. He might even be able to use some shorthand that she couldn't because she didn't know their shared culture.

"What changed your mind?" Ben asked. He pushed his plate to one side.

"There was a break-in in town. Cat and I happened to be on the street when it occurred. The break-in involved a guy I'd already talked to about Larry. And I saw two men flee."

Ben nodded. "And?"

"They weren't kids, Ben. I went after them. They were trained. They were ghosts."

Ben closed his eyes briefly, then swore. "What else?"

"The fact that he was here working on a book but hadn't told a soul what it was about. He might have been developing that story or building a case against some others involved in that crap. And given the men I saw running, I'm not prepared to dismiss a military connection."

Ben clearly didn't want to be eating, but he plugged away at it. Sometimes even the best food became a mere fuel.

After a couple more mouthfuls, Ben spoke again. "That would make sense. Awful, ugly sense. Damn it, Larry."

Duke just shook his head. "That was Larry. We both know it. I wouldn't be surprised if there were things he couldn't mention in his original story because he didn't have enough corroborating evidence or testimony. It also wouldn't surprise me if he couldn't let those loose ends go."

"He never would," Ben agreed. "Never. They'd have been driving him nuts until he found answers."

"Much as he could be a clam," Duke replied, "he was talking to people. Maybe some dangerous people."

"Didn't he always do that? Way of life for him." Ben

compressed his lips, his entire face tightening. Then, "You think they might be after me."

Cat spoke. "We can't ignore the possibility, Ben. They might be coming for Duke, too. Whoever they are, they probably aren't familiar with Larry's secrecy about his work. They might think that anyone who knew him might have information."

"But Larry kept us secret."

"There are always people who know," Duke said. "Always. Unless you were living in an isolated cave, someone would know you were close."

After they put the leftovers away, they repaired to the living room with coffee. No beer. Not now, as night began to fall in slow stages. Cat looked outside and saw the snow was still falling slowly but not yet sticking. She hadn't heard any other vehicles on the road out front, and from where she stood at the front window, she could see no signs of life.

But night approached, and the cover of darkness could bring threat.

If the break-ins were related to Larry's murder, the perps had spaced them out a bit. It should be too soon for another attempt.

By the same token, since Duke had chased those two guys, their timetable may have sped up. Or maybe the two intervening burglaries had merely been diversionary. Maybe they had their sights on bigger targets, like Duke and Ben.

Duke interrupted the heavy, tense silence. "I'm going to take a walk around the perimeter before it gets dark, maybe move the truck farther away so it doesn't pro-

vide concealment. You two button up the house. Curtains closed. Later we can turn out all the lights and
keep watch."

"Great evening," Cat said, winking at Ben.

He smiled faintly. "Oh yeah. Standing post. Love it."

During the passing hours, she had grown considerably more convinced that Duke had been right about
what was coming down. She hoped not, but her stance
was shifting. Maybe it helped that Ben had no problem believing the theory. She sure hoped she'd brought
what they'd need.

THE GROUND HADN'T yet become muddy from the snowflakes that melted as soon as they fell on it. It had, however, softened just a bit, silencing Duke's footsteps as
he slipped around to the back and began his patrol of
a wide perimeter. He didn't wear the goggles because
he wanted his full field of vision. Peripheral vision was
great at detecting movement.

Much as the early twilight messed with depth and
shadows, he could still see enough. The falling snowflakes amplified the remaining light. What he sought
was any evidence of someone having been out here
creeping around. This wasn't the kind of place a person
might take a casual walk. Too far away from anything
else, including other dwellings.

He also needed to scout the terrain. From a tactical
and strategic perspective, knowing the ground was essential. Where could a team hide when approaching
the house? How many significant ditches and dips lay

out here? Any formations large enough to hide behind? Easy approaches?

The tall evergreens that lined the property about three hundred feet from the house didn't worry him. They'd be temporary cover at best. But a gully deep enough to provide concealment for someone to approach the house? Big problem.

Each time he paused to view the ground, he looked back to the house, considering angles of attack, soft points to approach.

Because the first thing he'd done was move his rental truck down the driveway, so it was near the road, he didn't have to take care of that. Insofar as possible, it didn't announce that Ben had visitors. But mostly he didn't want to give them a place to hide.

Duke didn't want to scare them off. He wanted these creeps to come after Ben. He wanted to take them down. For Ben, because he deserved to live without fear, especially fear that his relationship with Larry had brought hell raining down on him. Larry wouldn't have wanted that, nor did Duke.

And of course he wanted justice for Larry. Assuming these guys were out here trying to bury something to protect brass or others back home, he might never get to the root cause of it. Not ever. Duke was resigned to that. What he wasn't resigned to was letting his brother's murderers get away with it, with letting them get away with all the other people they'd frightened.

Nope, time for justice.

Chapter Eleven

"We go tonight," Man One said.

The three of them huddled beneath the tall evergreens, more shadows among already deep shadows. The steadily falling snow magnified a little bit of light despite the darkness above. Enough to see by. Maybe too much. Man One was past caring.

"Are you serious?" asked the second man. "Damn it, I haven't even finished searching for the information on the computer or the flash drives. We might already have it."

"Yeah," agreed the third man. He'd seen plenty of action during his years in uniform and wasn't afraid of it. The only thing that truly scared him was stupidity. He didn't want to be stupid or to be led by it.

"The guy's there. He's sleeping. We can handle him and take our time to search."

Man Two bumped his head as he moved. A quiet curse escaped him. "What about that truck down by the end of the driveway? Somebody else is in that house. Just maybe."

"I don't freaking care," said the first man. "You two

wanna spend the rest of our lives out here hunting for something we can't find? You want to bring huge numbers of staties down on this place because we commit so many burglaries? At this point it's hardly likely that we'll have this gig much longer. They'll call us failures, refuse to pay what they owe us and send someone else out here."

"Sure," said the second man.

"It's a wild-goose chase," the third man agreed morosely. "I mean, damn! What if all the information was in Larry Duke's head? We're going on a lot of supposition here. Like, if he dumped a disc or a drive or a file on someone else that they'd even know what to make of it. They'd probably just trash it."

"Word," said the second man reluctantly.

"Exactly," said the first man. "The longer we're out here, the more I start wondering if someone isn't trying to get rid of the three of us."

Shocked silence greeted the words.

After a minute or so, Man Two asked, "Why would they want to do that?"

"Damned if I know. This whole op is so fishy I'm wondering how I ever got talked into it. Well, money, I guess. Retirement ain't so easy. But apart from that, it didn't sound so damn difficult. It *wasn't* difficult until Larry Duke said we'd never find the info. That's when it all blew up."

"True," the third man agreed. "I thought it would be simple, too."

"In and out," said the second man. "It should have been."

Instead...

Man Two stirred again. "But they have no reason to get rid of us."

"Now they do," the first man said grimly. "From the minute we interrogated Duke, we screwed up. Made a mess. Even if we get out of here, we're in trouble. Somebody might worry that we'll be found out and can spill the beans."

"What beans?" demanded the third man. "We don't have any beans!"

"I do," said the first man. "I talk to the boss. Why would anyone think I haven't told you who that is?"

"Aw, hell."

"Exactly," said the first man. "We're in it now. Whichever way we go. So tonight we go into that house, search it, then get the hell out of this state."

"But what if there's another man in there?"

"Then I hope it's Daniel Duke," said the first man.

"You got a grudge?"

"Now I do."

The other two had no idea what that meant, but they weren't going to ask. They were stuck and figured the first guy would shoot them both in the back if they refused to follow him.

Things sure changed when you were up to no good.

THE THREE INSIDE the house had agreed to spell each other on lookout duty, allowing the others to take naps. They'd opened the curtains at one window on each side of the house. The idea was to give themselves a full view of outside approaches without allowing anyone to scope the entire indoors from out there. The night seemed to devour the inside of the house, little light to break up the darkness. The only glimmer they had at all was reflected by the falling snow through the uncovered windows.

Each of them took turns walking window to window to keep an eye on the land surrounding the house. The night-vision goggles that Cat had brought helped. Reasonably clear, green-tinged images made the house safely passable indoors and gave a clear view of the world outside the windows.

And it was boring, Cat thought as she wandered window to window, riot gun in hand, peering out into the night. Those guys probably had goggles, too, if they were what Duke suspected.

Well, if they showed up, at least they wouldn't have an advantage.

There'd been little time for it yet, but her mind kept trying to wander back to her lovemaking with Duke. She wanted to replay every detail repeatedly on an infinite loop. Except she couldn't remember a lot of it.

She almost giggled at herself. She'd been so swept away at the time, she'd hardly been aware of anything besides the stormy sea of emotions.

Now this. Life had been rushing by. Too many things to think about, to worry about. No time for wandering through dreams.

Nor could she afford to indulge now. The lives of others depended on her being alert, not dopey.

She heard a creak on the stairs in the hallway behind her and turned to see Duke descending. "Cat," he said quietly.

"You're supposed to be sleeping."

"I rarely sleep well on a night op. Doesn't matter.

Morning will come, and I'll feel like a fool for putting everyone through this."

She pushed her goggles up, then realized that could be a mistake. Without their light amplification, total darkness surrounded her. "You're not a fool. And you know they might not come tonight. What matters is that we're here to look after Ben if he needs us."

"And tomorrow night?"

She shook her head. "I already told you. I'm going to insist he come into town and stay at my place. Out here he's hanging in the wind."

He caught her chin with his fingers. "You're a great person, Cat."

"Right now I'm not being a very good sentry."

He laughed quietly. "I can see over your shoulder, Deputy. But you go cadge some sleep. I'll take over."

"No." She turned from him reluctantly and looked out the window. "We're getting to the witching hour. Two sets of eyes would be better."

"Witching hour?" he asked. "I thought that was midnight."

"For this, I'd bet it's more like 2:00 a.m. As the world falls into its deepest sleep."

"Those were the hours we preferred for operations," he agreed. "I just thought 'the witching hour' referred to something else."

"It might. I don't know." She pulled her goggles down, treating herself to a few seconds of looking at him, then started her patrol again.

"Stay back from the windows," he reminded her.

Yeah. Stay back because the guys out there might have night vision, too, and could catch sight of movement in here. And why had she started to grow so tense? A tightening through her muscles, the back of her neck prickling. Well, she *was* edgy.

A level playing field? She didn't think so. Those guys could move freely out there. Here inside, she and the two men were practically caged.

"I'll do the far side of the house," Duke said quietly. "More eyes on. We can start switching off every half hour."

"Yeah." She paused. "When you did your recon, did you find any features that concerned you?"

"Actually, yeah. From the kitchen side of the house. There's a gully that could be deep enough to conceal crawling men. Assuming the snow doesn't start to stick. Then it all becomes different out there."

Considering how much light was being reflected by the snowflakes that fell almost lazily, she couldn't imagine what it would all look like under a white blanket out there. They might not even need the goggles from in here.

Unless someone managed to get inside.

"We need to get Ben," she said before Duke could disappear to the other side of the house. "I don't know why, but my skin is crawling."

"He's already watching from upstairs."

"Oh." So much for them taking turns.

Duke faced her. "Your skin is crawling? Like somebody's watching?"

"Imagination, maybe. I'm wound up. It only just started, though."

His reply was quick. "Don't ignore it. I never do."

He headed for the kitchen side of the house, and she

resumed her patrol, easing to each window, minimizing any quickness of movement that might draw attention if someone was out there watching.

She looked out that same window again, wondering. Was someone looking in? She hadn't noticed any movement, but she'd been distracted for a minute or two with Duke. Bad. Thank goodness Ben had decided to forgo sleep.

Sentry duty had to be the worst assignment in the world. Things creeping in the dark, a threat possibly looming and weariness making it even harder to stay alert.

TWENTY MINUTES LATER, Duke thought he caught sight of movement in the direction of that ditch that had snagged his attention. These guys, whoever they were, didn't think anyone was watching for them. Reasonable stealth, but not the best.

He peered more intently, waiting for a second movement before he sounded an alert. No point ramping everyone up if all he'd seen was a small animal.

Five minutes later, he was sure. More than one thing moved out there, and they were spreading out slowly. Three.

He couldn't leave the window, needing to keep an eye on the three moving lumps, waiting for the image to clear up, and tried to judge how loudly to warn the others.

He didn't need to. Ben came clattering down the stairs.

"Something's moving," Ben said tautly. "Kitchen side."

"Eyes on," Duke answered. "It may not all be on this side of the house. Cat? You hear?"

"I heard."

Duke looked at Ben. "Are they just planning a break-in? Or an assault?"

Ben shook his head a bit. "I don't have an assessment. I keep thinking of Larry. That was no simple break-in."

"No. We'll keep watching, but get ready for an assault. We need to know how many are out there."

Cat joined them briefly. "I don't see anything from my side, but I'll go back to watching." She hurried away.

"Why would there be so many?" Ben wondered. "Three? More than three? What are they doing, raiding Fort Knox?"

"Maybe," Duke said heavily, "they don't figure you're alone."

FOR THE THREE men crawling across the ground to the house, the situation had become clearer. There was more than one person in there, and they were moving around. Not much, but they were still moving. A glimpse here and there spelled it out.

They were prepared to take out everyone if they needed to. Even if they never found the information, they'd have eliminated the one person who might know anything at all about what Larry was doing: his partner.

That thought made the first man's gorge rise, but he was a realist. The first person a guy was likely to spill classified info to was his wife. In fact, the military wives' grapevine was legendary.

Had to be the same for two guys, reasoned Man One.

And if Daniel Duke was in there, so much the better. He hated Duke. Had hated him since the man had shown up armed to the teeth to rescue the first man's squad. Single-handedly. Risking life and limb to do it.

Duke hadn't needed to come. Man One still believed he could have handled it, but no. Man One had come out of it feeling like he'd been punched, and people had talked about Duke getting the Medal of Honor for saving a pinned-down squad like some kind of screaming avenger. In the face of extremely heavy fire. Duke had been wounded, but he'd still managed to drag two of the wounded soldiers to safety and take out most of the insurgent nest.

Sounded real good for Duke. Man One didn't quite remember it that way. His squad could have handled it. Would have handled it.

His bitterness had been slightly assuaged by the fact that Duke and he had both received the same commendation for that action. But not completely assuaged, because Man One should have received all the kudos. All of them.

Being told to come after Larry Duke had been one of Man One's deciding factors when he accepted this assignment. It might also have given him an additional reason to torture Larry.

He wouldn't think about that now.

He had a mission to accomplish.

DUKE WOULD HAVE liked to get outside for an improved view of what was happening. He knew better, however. He'd alert those men and probably become their first target.

Given that they were creeping up so slowly, he was doubting more and more that they'd come merely to rob the place. No, they were staging an action, they knew Ben wasn't alone and they didn't intend to leave anyone behind.

He could feel his scalp prickle and his shoulders tighten. The battle was about to begin. He just hoped they could stop those guys before things grew truly ugly.

Another movement caught his eye, and he stared at it, for the first time seeing a silhouette that looked like an assault rifle. They were arriving with heavy firepower. Bad news.

He called to the other two, "Getting closer. Armed. Watch it. They may spread out more to encircle the house." He checked his clip. The shotguns were ready.

Another minute or two crept by. Then one man rose up, leveled his rifle and fired.

The bullet zinged through the window Duke faced. War had been declared.

"Here we go," he called out. "Stay low, stay alert." As if they wouldn't. They had to have heard the shot.

And those men had just given up any hope of surprise. Which meant they knew someone was aware of them. Which meant they didn't care but were prepared to take extreme action.

The question was, were they expecting the kind of greeting they were about to get?

CAT JOINED DUKE at the kitchen window. "Have they divided?" she asked quietly.

"They're starting to. You take the front window, unless you want me to."

"I'm thinking about firing right now. A warning shot. No reason they have to get any closer."

He looked at her quickly before looking back out. Were they trying to set a trap or put an end to this?

He reconsidered. Yeah, a trap would be nice, as it would separate them, but a whole lot more dangerous.

"Okay," he said. "When you catch sight of one near the front, fire away, identify yourself and tell them to stop. Ben and I will deal with what happens then."

"Fair enough."

Outside, apparently emboldened when their shot didn't receive return fire, the men rose up, crouching, but much more visible. Two headed toward the front, which meant they intended to enter. Why was that one staying on the side?

But his question was quickly answered. The last of them started to move toward the front. He watched, then joined Cat and Ben in the foyer.

"They're here," Cat announced. "I'm going ahead."

Ben reached out swiftly. "Be careful."

"I'm not going out there," she said reassuringly. She then opened the door a crack and put her mouth to the opening.

"Conard County Sheriff. Freeze right there!"

But they didn't even hesitate. *Cripes*, she thought, raising the shotgun and edging it through the door. She fired a warning blast.

"I said halt!" She fired again.

She felt one of the guys push some more shells into her hand and she quickly loaded them, for the first time wishing she'd brought magazines. Who would have guessed? She'd honestly believed that a few warning shots would stop them. If not, a couple more well-placed shots should have done it.

But nothing was stopping these men.

Then the rain of fire began.

The three of them swore and fell to the floor. Automatics, Cat thought. No three-round bursts to preserve ammo, so they must have plenty.

The bullets came through the entire front of the house, as if they wanted to saw it down, and ricocheted off metal or punctured the walls and staircase. Glass shattered.

"Let me," Duke said, edging her to one side.

"Careful," she couldn't help saying, although he didn't need the reminder. He was far more experienced at this than she'd ever be.

Ben cried out as more bullets pierced the house.

"Ben?" she called.

"A graze. Damn it. I can't lift my arm…"

Just then, Duke rose on his knees, pushed the door open wider and fired into the night. A single crack.

Almost simultaneously a man's cry could be heard.

"One down," Duke said. "Hang on."

Cat rose up. Without asking, she hurried over to the broken front window and used the butt of her shotgun to get more glass out of the way. Then she aimed for one of the attackers.

Enough, she thought. *Enough. This one's for Larry.* Her heart pounded in her ears, and rage filled her.

Another swath of bullets cut through, and she had to duck, but then she rose up and fired another round. A riot gun wasn't particular. Nor was she, at this point.

All the while fear tapped along her spine. Fear that Ben had been downplaying his injury. Fear that Duke would get shot.

Her own safety was the last thing that worried her. Strange.

Must have been the fury.

TEN MINUTES AFTER the firefight began, it ended in total silence. Eerie silence.

Cat felt almost dazed as she tried to look around.

"I need to go out there and check," Duke said. "You help Ben."

"No," said Ben. "I'll be fine. I managed to put on a tourniquet."

Cat looked at Duke. "You're not going out there alone. They're still armed, and if any of them can shoot…"

"It's common tactical sense, Duke," Ben argued. "Don't go alone."

Duke was having none of it. "Cat, you stay here with Ben. He can't defend himself. I'll deal with those three. Quite effectively."

Then he slipped out the door.

Ben spoke as if in answer to Cat's instant anxiety. "If anyone can do it, he can."

CAT WISHED SHE could see more. The night-vision goggles were displaying all kinds of static as the snowfall grew heavier.

She thought she saw Duke moving slowly toward the three men. Then a volley of shots rang out. Her heart stopped.

One man must be capable of shooting. At least one.

While the subsequent silence seemed to last forever, it didn't. She knew it didn't.

Ben spoke, his voice weaker. "Cat? What's going on?"

"Damned if I know."

The anxiety was going to kill her. One dark figure began to move toward the house. She lifted her shotgun, ready to fire, then recognized Duke's familiar stride.

She could have collapsed with relief. With her radio, now certain no one else would get hurt, she called for help and relief.

Not too long after, the two medevac choppers arrived. The first one took Ben. The second took two of the wounded men. The other was dead.

The medics had flex ties and used them on the two shooters. They'd survive, but no one was taking a chance that they could cause more trouble.

Cat, knowing Ben would receive the best care, joined Duke, who was looking at the man who lay dead on the ground, the snow starting to collect on his clothing. The dead man was on his back, his eyes open and fixed on night he could no longer see.

"He shot at you?" she asked. "You shot him?"

"Yeah." Duke's voice was heavy. Then he said, "I know him."

A shiver of shock ran through Cat. "You do?"

"Yeah. Years back, we were both in the 'Stan. I was on a solo mission when I heard a firefight. I had my own mission, and maybe I should have ignored it, but…" He shook his head. "I couldn't," he said simply.

Cat waited, still trying to deal with the hurricane that buffeted her. "And?" she asked after a minute.

"Oh, I found a squad under attack. Some wounded guys, and it didn't look good for them. I got involved." He indicated the corpse with his hand. "He was leading them. I thought at the time that he wasn't happy I showed up, but that wasn't the point. Those wounded men were. I helped. Dragged the wounded guys to safer ground and joined the fight."

"You did that under fire?"

"Hell, yeah. Bad situation. No reason the wounded should become target practice."

"But why would he be here now?"

Duke just shook his head.

It seemed like a weird confluence, Cat thought, but stranger coincidences happened. Random, unexpected things.

The patrol cars had begun arriving, and soon Gage limped toward them, his shearling jacket hanging open, a tan cowboy hat on his head. He looked down at the corpse then at Cat. "Explain quickly, then get home. You can fill out reports tomorrow."

"Three armed men approached the house and started to make Swiss cheese out of it. We returned fire. Ben was wounded. Two of the intruders were as well. This one wasn't that lucky."

Gage turned his head. "The house doesn't look very good."

Understatement of the year, Cat thought. "I should go back inside, get anything Ben might want."

"Make it quick," Gage said.

She hurried back inside, looking around. She doubted Ben would want any clothes before tomorrow, but then she spied a photo of Ben and Larry together. Framed, it had been protected behind glass that was now shattered. She took it. Broken glass or not, she could put it beside his hospital bed.

"Now go," Gage said. "Both of you. We'll talk tomorrow. Leave the weapons behind and let us get to work. This is one thing I don't need you for, Cat."

She didn't even want to argue. As the adrenaline began to wear off, she began to feel wrung out, limp. Exhausted.

She and Duke didn't say much on the drive back. Too soon for an after-action report, she thought. Both of them needed time to absorb it all.

But that bit about knowing one of the guys, a man he'd assisted in Afghanistan, must have rocked him. He was probably sitting behind the wheel chewing that over. He hadn't struck her as a man who easily accepted coincidence as a reason.

Maybe he was right. She just hoped he wasn't blaming himself for Larry.

DUKE DROVE STRAIGHT to the truck stop. Cat, now dozing, hardly stirred as he went inside to order up two loaded breakfasts and a half gallon of coffee. If she could go to bed when they got to her house, that was fine by him. He doubted he'd be able to.

Not until he pulled up in front of her house did she actually wake. Then she yawned and stretched, and he watched with mild amusement as she staggered toward her front door. Yeah, it was still the middle of the night, but he suspected she was having a physical letdown. Just wait until that passed. She was going to be all over the night, the entire case, when she had the brainpower.

She made it inside. When he followed with the take-out bags and the tray full of coffee cups, he was astonished to find her sitting at the kitchen table. She rested her chin in her hand, her eyelids at half-staff.

"Go to bed," he suggested. "You're beat."

She shook her head slowly. "It's hitting."

"Thought it would. Then join me for breakfast."

"Sorry I fell asleep."

Duke paused as he pulled out the containers and offered her one of the coffees. "I'm not. I wouldn't have been much company. Besides, you were coming off adrenaline. I know what that's like."

"But not tonight?" she asked groggily as he opened boxes and put one in front of her, along with a fork. She blinked. "Did you get everything?"

"On the breakfast menu. We need the calories."

She nodded and speared a home fry, carrying it to her mouth. "Probably."

They ate quietly for a while, but Duke knew the questions were going to come, probably the same ones he had. As the fuel hit their systems, they would both reenergize.

When they were finally sated, he pushed the nearly empty containers aside and handed out two more cups of coffee.

"Is it still snowing?" Cat asked.

"It stopped while we were driving home."

She nodded and let out a big sigh. She began to turn the foam cup in front of her. "I need to get an espresso maker."

That comment came from so far out of left field that Duke felt taken aback. Was she still half-asleep? Or was she not ready to deal with the night's events yet?

Either way, he didn't blame her and just let her sit and settle. He knew her too well already to believe stasis would last long. He'd also been through enough situations like this to understand that some people needed longer to crawl back inside their own skins.

Besides, he was trying not to deal with a larger picture that kept occurring to him.

"We need to go see Ben," she announced.

"Rest a little. Ben's probably pretty busy about now."

"Did you see his wound?"

"Upper arm, tourniquet. Bad enough, I suspect. But he'll be fine. He just needs some stitches and maybe a shot of morphine."

Cat nodded.

Duke waited, his mind buzzing like a hive of bees. Not a coincidence. Couldn't be.

Cat sighed again and drank quite a bit of coffee before speaking. "You knew that guy?"

"Not really. We only ran into each other that once. But the minute I saw him, I knew who he was."

And every time he remembered that, his gut twisted in a knot. Had that man turned Larry into a proxy target? God, he hoped not. That was the only thing that could make this worse.

Cat stirred. "I hate to say this, but I can't deal with this right now. Maybe in the morning."

Which was how they came to be snuggled together under the covers. Just hugging. Duke had never found such comfort after any action. Wasn't supposed to need it.

Right then, he discovered that he *did* need it.

ALL TOO SOON, the day began. Cat awoke shortly after Duke, and the two of them headed straight to Community Memorial Hospital, Cat carrying the shattered photo of Larry and Ben.

Cat wore her uniform, and that got them past any gatekeepers.

"Ben needs some family here," Cat said under her breath.

"Yeah," Duke agreed. "I think they all disowned him, though."

"Damn."

"Larry used to laugh it off, without mentioning Ben by name, saying he'd never have an in-law problem. Honestly, I don't think either of them was able to really laugh it off."

"I couldn't."

Ben sat up in bed, eating from a tray of food that looked more appetizing than it probably was. He offered a weary smile. "Cooked prunes, anyone? Oatmeal? I've always hated oatmeal."

"Me, too," Cat answered. "Sticks in my mouth." She held out the photo. "I thought you might want this. Careful of the broken glass."

Ben took it and looked down at it. "That shattered glass feels like my heart."

She was sure it did.

"How are you doing?" Duke asked him.

"Nicked the brachial artery. Tourniquet saved me." He gave a snort. "Military training can be good for something."

"It appears," Duke agreed.

Ben continued to stare down at the photo. Then he ran his hand over the backing, as if stroking it. He'd probably have stroked the photo if it had been safe to do so.

Then his hand froze. "I've held this a million times in the past," he said slowly.

Duke leaned forward. "What's wrong?"

"There's something behind the backing. Something that wasn't there when I first put it in the house." He looked up, his eyes wide. "Duke?"

Duke looked at Cat. "Maybe you should take it."

She nodded. Evidence of some kind? Or just damage from the firefight last night? Only one way to find out.

She placed the photo facedown on the table, then felt the backing carefully. It rocked slightly. Picture backing, no matter how thick, didn't usually do that.

Carefully, she bent back the tabs that held it in place. "I'll remove the glass once I can get the photo out."

"Sure," Ben said.

She could feel both men watching intently. Her heart was climbing into her throat. At last she was able to lift the backing off—and what she saw caused her breath to catch.

"What?" both men asked.

She slowly lifted out three discs in their paper sleeves and held them up. "Could these be it? Larry's secret?"

Chapter Twelve

Four days later they stood in Good Shepherd Church for Larry's memorial. Cat hadn't expected much of a turnout, given that Larry had barely arrived in town and Ben was still only slightly known.

But the church was packed.

She smiled faintly, glad to see it. Ben needed to feel community support right now. Support even from relative strangers.

The last few days had been tough for both Ben and Duke. Enough details of the autopsy had been shared to give both men a crystal clear awareness of what had been done to Larry. The minimum, but still too much. At least neither of them had pressed for more information, although they could have.

Rocked by that, Duke had nonetheless forged ahead, working with Ben on a service for his brother while keeping his finger on the pulse of the interrogation of the two men who had survived their assault on Ben's house.

It seemed someone had hired the men to come out here to remove any evidence Larry might have of misdeeds among higher-ups in the Army relating to the murder-for-hire plot. The information was on those discs—lots of it. Names, dates, places, witnesses. It would indeed have filled a book.

Duke planned to turn it over to military authorities for investigation, but not before he asked the sheriff to make copies for safekeeping. A chain of evidence.

In addition, they'd found out that the dead man, Jason Lewis, had a burr under his saddle about Duke.

"When he heard you were in town," one of the killers said, "he started to go kinda nuts. I don't know why."

The other man did. "Just before we began that attack, he told me that Major Duke had interfered with an operation of his in Afghanistan."

Questions answered, Cat thought as she waited for Reverend Carson to make her appearance. It wasn't often that *all* the questions got answered.

Ben had decided he wanted Larry buried nearby. He also wanted to give the eulogy. Duke seemed content to be guided.

When Ben rose, his arm in a sling, his eyes were visibly wet. "I planned to say a whole lot, but somehow I can't. Larry was one of the good guys, always a warrior for justice, unafraid in the teeth of death threats. A hard-driving reporter who always wanted the truth and wouldn't settle for less."

Ben's voice broke, and he dashed at his eyes, wiping away tears.

Cat's throat tightened, and she had to blink herself.

"Anyway, maybe Larry's brother can do a better job of this than I can. But I just wanted to say, I love Larry. I loved him since the first time we met. And I was hoping when he came out here, we'd start a real life together. We weren't granted the time, but…"

His voice broke again as he stuffed his hand into his pocket. When he drew it out, he held a gold ring.

"I was going to ask Larry to marry me." He laid the ring atop Larry's casket and walked down the steps toward the aisle.

Then the most beautiful thing happened. People rose from the pews and surrounded him, offering hugs and kind words. Offering him a sense of belonging, a sense that his grief was shared.

Cat couldn't hold back the tears any longer.

MUCH LATER, CAT, Ben and Duke gathered in her living room. It had been a wrenching day for all of them, especially the men. First the service, then the trip to the cemetery. Then a funeral supper back at the church, where a whole lot of friendly people delivered a potluck.

Now they kicked back with beers and let all the grief and fatigue wash over them.

"Larry loved what he did," Ben said. "I would never have asked him to stop. He was made for that job."

"I agree," said Duke. "Definitely. A remarkable guy, and I don't just say that because he's my brother."

"He said that about you, too." Ben smiled faintly.

After a few minutes of reflection, Duke looked at Cat. "I know this is quick, but it's driving me crazy. Would you consider marrying me eventually? I love you."

Cat caught her breath. *Seriously?*

Then Duke turned to Ben. "If she says yes, will you be my best man?"

For the first time since the murder, Ben smiled broadly. "I wouldn't miss it."

Then the two men looked at Cat, who was bouncing between amazement and joy. "Are both of you asking?"

"Seems like," said Duke. "One big family now. If you want."

Oh, truth rushed through her. No deliberation or time needed. "I want," she breathed. "Yes, definitely yes."

A bright ray of sunshine filled her, warming her.

So much joy out of so much sorrow. Life could still be beautiful.

And justice could still be served.

* * * * *

Don't miss other romances in Rachel Lee's thrilling Conard County: The Next Generation series:

Stalked in Conard County
Murdered in Conard County
Conard County Watch
Conard County Revenge

Available now from Harlequin!

COMING NEXT MONTH FROM

⒣ HARLEQUIN

INTRIGUE

Available May 19, 2020

HICNM0520

Prologue

They warned him not to go to the police.

He couldn't think. Couldn't breathe.

Forcing one foot in front of the other, he tried to ignore the gut-
wrenching pain at the base of his skull where the kidnapper had
slammed him into his kitchen floor and knocked him unconscious.
Owen. Olivia. They were out there. Alone. Scared. He hadn't been
strong enough to protect them, but he wasn't going to stop trying to
find them. Not until he got them back.

A wave of dizziness tilted the world on its axis, and he collided
with a wooden street pole. Shoulder-length hair blocked his vision
as he fought to regain balance. He'd woken up a little less than
fifteen minutes ago, started chasing after the taillights of the SUV
as it'd sped down the unpaved road leading into town. He could still
taste the dirt in his mouth. They couldn't have gotten far. Someone
had to have seen something...

Humidity settled deep into his lungs despite the dropping
temperatures, sweat beading at his temples as he pushed himself

upright. Moonlight beamed down on him, exhaustion pulling at every muscle in his body, but he had to keep going. He had to find his kids. They were all he had left. All that mattered.

Colorless worn mom-and-pop stores lining the town's main street blurred in his vision.

A small group of teenagers—at least what looked like teenagers—gathered around a single point on the sidewalk ahead. The kidnapper had sped into town from his property just on the outskirts, and there were only so many roads that would get the bastard out. Maybe someone in the group could point him in the right direction. He latched on to a kid brushing past him by the collar. "Did you see a black SUV speed through here?"

The boy—sixteen, seventeen—shook his head and pulled away. "Get off me, man."

The echo of voices pierced through the ringing in his ears as the circle of teens closed in on itself in front of Sevierville's oldest hardware store. His lungs burned with shallow breaths as he searched the streets from his position in the middle of the sidewalk. Someone had to have seen something. Anything. He needed—

"She's bleeding!" a girl said. "Someone call for an ambulance!"

The hairs on the back of his neck stood on end. Someone had been hurt? Pushing through the circle of onlookers, he caught sight of pink pajama pants and bright purple toenails. He surrendered to the panic as recognition flared. His heart threatened to burst straight out of his chest as he lunged for the unconscious six-year-old girl sprawled across the pavement. Pain shot through his knees as he scooped her into his arms. "Olivia!"

Don't miss
Midnight Abduction *by Nichole Severn,*
available June 2020 wherever
Harlequin Intrigue books and ebooks are sold.

Harlequin.com